GUSTY LOVERS AND CADAVERS

A RAINA SUN MYSTERY

ANNE R. TAN

*To Rhys,
for helping me understand men*

BABY ON BOARD

Raina was smart enough to know a Jiggle Me doll for the baby of the family wasn't enough to ease her cousins' animosity over the lawsuit contesting their grandfather's will. After all, it wasn't her fault the cousins only got one dollar each, and she got three million, but she had to try. For her grandma's sake.

She glanced at the sliding glass doors to the entrance of Bullseye. The Christmas music piping through hidden speakers grated on her nerves as she waited by the display case between the restrooms and Starbucks cafe. The yuletide song didn't appear to make the shoppers any less desperate for the hot gift of the season. In fact, it probably just reminded everyone this was the last shopping weekend before D-day.

"Oh, Raina, you don't have to. It's not our tradition to give presents, and money is tight for you," said Cassie over the phone.

"I have this housekeeping gig at a fancy resort for winter break. I'll be fine. Besides, Lila is my only niece. I'm here shopping with the foreign exchange student anyway. Or I will be when she gets here."

"One toy, but that's it. See you at the Christmas dinner."

Raina hung up and glanced at the entrance of the store again. She normally wasn't a stickler for punctuality, but Fanny was forty minutes late and hadn't even bothered sending a text message. Raina had given up Saturday morning brunch with her grandma to take the foreign exchange student shopping.

So a trip to the big box retail store wasn't exactly "shopping," but it was more convenient than traipsing through the mom-and-pop stores in downtown Gold Springs or driving to Sacramento. Either option would have taken up her entire afternoon. It wasn't like Fanny would know any different. Or at least Raina hoped she didn't.

"Excuse me," said a thickly accented voice from behind her.

Raina turned. "Yes?"

The pixie-faced Chinese woman bit her lower lip. Her eyes darted nervously over Raina's shoulder. The baby cradled in her arms slept as only an infant could with all the noise in the store.

Raina glanced over her shoulder but couldn't tell what the young mom was looking at. She squinted at another Chinese woman exiting the store. Did the woman have pink highlights like the foreign exchange student? "Fanny!" She waved an arm. "Hey, Fanny! Over here!" The woman didn't turn around. Oops, wrong person.

Something soft and warm pressed against her other arm. She whipped her head around to stare at the stranger who held out her baby with both hands.

"Can you hold baby for me? I need use potty. No place put baby inside."

Raina took a step back, her arms held out automatically to ward off the intrusion into her personal space. "Have we met?"

This was the strangest proposition she'd gotten in a while. Didn't this woman know she shouldn't trust a stranger with her child?

The woman pointed at the short hall next to them. "Potty." She shook her head and made a buckling motion as if putting on a seat belt. "No place for baby."

Raina assumed she meant there wasn't a working baby changing station in the restroom stall. Cassie had often complained how difficult it was to pee while juggling a baby in a public restroom the few times she ran out of the house for quick trips without her stroller.

The woman's tailored clothes and Coach purse suggested she should have money to buy a stroller. Even the baby was clad in an expensive blue cashmere one-piece. Or they could be knock-offs? Not that Raina could tell otherwise.

"I trust you with most precious gift: my son." Her eyes widened as if she just had an important thought. "My name Sui Yuk Liang. What your name, please?" She dropped the huge diaper bag next to Raina's feet.

The conversation was beginning to have a surreal quality to it. "Raina Sun." She glanced at the automatic sliding glass doors at the front of the store. Still no Fanny.

Sui Yuk nodded as if the exchange of their names solidified her trust. "Rain Water. You Chinese like me. You take care baby." She thrust the child into Raina's arms and released her hold.

Raina caught the infant. It was either that or the child would kiss the floor. Before she could utter a word, Sui Yuk disappeared into the hallway toward the women's restroom. Raina tucked the infant against her shoulder, cradling his head. How did she get herself into these situations? First Fanny and now this.

She should be more gracious and welcoming toward the foreign exchange student, but the couple of times she'd spent in Fanny's company hadn't left her with warm fuzzy feelings. This favor was for her friend Brenda, who was too busy dealing with the Christmas orders for pies and cakes at the Venus Cafe.

As the host family, Brenda or her husband, Joe, should be the ones helping Fanny with her shopping. But when Brenda asked if Raina could help out since she was close in age to Fanny, she had to say yes. She couldn't jeopardize her special status as a friend of the owners. The food was that good. And so was the discount.

Did ten o'clock mean something different in China? Not that Raina would know. The bus ride to Bullseye was straightforward and only took twenty minutes. She wouldn't have agreed to meet Fanny at the store otherwise. If Fanny didn't show up soon, Raina would have to spend her lunch trying to track down the foreign exchange student. What was that Chinese proverb? Duty was heavier than a mountain.

She glanced at the hall. Five more minutes and then she'd pop her head in the restroom. Did Sui Yuk have a diarrhea attack? She didn't want to embarrass the young mom, but this would explain her desperate willingness to trust a stranger to watch her baby while she did the dirty deed.

"I was here first," said an irritated male voice.

Raina glanced at the mile-long line at Starbucks.

A middle-aged man with a receding hairline glared at the barista behind the counter.

"I have been waiting for the last fifteen minutes." He pointed a tapered finger at the young woman stirring sugar into her cup. "She was behind me. Why did she get her coffee before me?"

Raina rolled her eyes. The holidays brought out everyone's best behavior.

The baby grunted and wiggled. Time to find the baby's mama.

She hooked the diaper bag on one shoulder and made her way into the women's restroom. The diaper bag was heavier than Atlas's burden and just as bulky. Her left shoulder already ached from carrying it. "Deck the Halls" echoed between the stalls. She sidestepped around the two women waiting in line and ignored their frowns.

"Sui Yuk," Raina whispered into the first stall. "Are you almost done? The baby is waking up."

No answer.

She repeated her performance at the next stall.

"Go away."

"Merry Christmas to you, too," Raina muttered.

The woman in the next stall answered with a curt, "Not here."

Raina knocked on the last stall. Sweat beaded on the small of her back as an uneasy feeling twisted in her gut. "Sui Yuk, are you in here? The baby is waking up."

"Wrong stall, hon," the woman called out.

Raina must have crossed paths with Sui Yuk somehow. She left the restroom and hustled back to the front of the store. Her eyes scanned the area, but she didn't see the mother anywhere. The baby started to root at her shoulder, making small ah-ah grunts. She patted his small back and prayed he would go back to sleep.

She trotted over to Guest Services and asked the attendant to page Sui Yuk.

The sleepy-eyed teenage guy shrugged. "Okay, madam." He made the announcement over the P.A. system and turned to help another customer.

The baby pumped his fists as he opened his mouth and wailed. A loud squawk as if he knew a stranger held him. Other customers were now staring openly as they walked by.

Food. The baby must need food. Raina dropped the diaper bag on the floor and dug around for a bottle. No milk. Her armpits dampened as a hot flash of anxiety ran through her. What mother would leave home without a bottle? Geez, even if Sui Yuk was nursing, she should come back before her baby needed to eat.

Raina fumbled to unzip a small side pocket and pulled out a sheet of wrinkled notebook paper. Her eyes widened at the words.

PLEASE CALL **758-1889** IF SOMETHING HAPPENS TO SUI YUK LIANG

What a strange note, she thought.

Bouncing the baby, she dialed the number, but it went straight to voicemail with a generic message to leave a callback number. Her message came out in a rush about Sui Yuk's failure to reappear after using the restroom. She left her name and both her home and cell phone numbers, wincing at the panic in her voice.

She clutched her phone and stared at the display. *Please call back.*

The baby's shriek pierced the area as if Raina held him over a boiling cauldron. She cradled his body and stuck her pinkie in his mouth. He sucked eagerly, but his tiny face crumbled as he realized her pinkie held no sustenance.

Maybe he didn't need food. Raina pulled the child closer and sniffed his diaper. Powder fresh. Her breath came out in a rush, grateful for the small favor.

Raina scanned the crowd again. No Sui Yuk appeared to claim her baby. Surely, a mother wouldn't just abandon her baby with a stranger.

She pressed her cell phone between her ear and shoulder as she bounced the child on her other shoulder. "Matthew, I'm holding a wailing baby, and I seem to have lost his mother." She ignored the pointed looks from the other shoppers and explained the situation.

Matthew Louie was a homicide detective, but she didn't know who else to call. And with a police force of only ten people, including the chief, it really didn't matter who she called. This would eventually make its way to the officer in charge of child abandonment cases.

The baby wiggled, and her phone slipped from her shoulder. It smashed onto the floor, and the back cover popped off. The battery slid across the white tiled floor and under the rows of shopping carts in front of her.

"Great!" she said to no one in particular.

She tucked the crying baby firmly into her arm and dropped to her knees. As she patted the space underneath the shopping carts, she was conscious of her butt-in-the-air pose.

"Rainy, why aren't you wearing the new underwear I got you? Your old ones leave too many panty lines," a familiar voice said from behind her.

Someone snickered.

Raina straightened and shifted the baby to her other shoulder to even out the ringing in her ears. "Real funny, Grandma. I'm dying here."

Po Po glanced at the wailing infant. She smiled at the child, her face becoming a roadmap of laugh lines in a cloud of silver hair. The baby's mouth opened and closed like a fish.

"You do know a baby is not like a cute dog. He's not going to be a conversation starter with men," her grandma said.

"I could use a hand here," Raina said through gritted teeth. As soon as the baby heard her voice, he started crying again. Her body tensed, and heat rushed to her face.

"Let me have the little one." Her grandma held the infant against one shoulder, shushing and swaying her body from side to side. The child relaxed and a finger found its way to his mouth.

Raina's eyes widened at the sight, but she didn't waste an extra second to stare at the contrast between the pink-faced baby and the white-haired elderly Chinese woman. She shoved the shopping carts aside to rescue her elusive battery.

The screen on her phone had a large crack across one corner. Her heart sank at the damage. She'd replaced her phone only a few months ago. Assembling the phone was a breeze, but the screen remained stubbornly black when she powered it on.

"Here. Use my smarty-pants phone," said Po Po.

Raina called Matthew again but got his voicemail this time. She left a brief message with her location and handed the phone back to her grandma.

"Keep it for now in case he calls back," said Po Po.

"What are you doing here? Miss spending your Saturday mornings with your favorite granddaughter?"

"My grandkids are like my toes. It's kind of hard to pick one to chop off." Po Po shifted the baby to her other shoulder. "So where is the famous foreign exchange student? I figured you'd bring her here since Sacramento is a little out of the way. I thought we could still have lunch after you're done." Po Po glanced at the baby. "But I didn't realize you would acquire a baby. Rainy, you're supposed to find a husband first. The baby comes later."

"Ha ha. You're a riot. She's a no-show. Right now, I have more important things to worry about, like finding out what happened to the baby's mother." Raina told her grandma what happened with Sui Yuk Liang.

"Why did you accept the baby? He's cute and all, but if you had said no, then you wouldn't be in this predicament."

Raina sighed. "Because he reminds me of Lila. I would hope if Cassie were ever in a similar situation, someone would help her like I helped Sui Yuk Liang. What would you have done?"

"Exactly what you did. Come on, Rainy. Let me buy you a drink."

The knot in Raina's stomach loosened, and the tension drained from her body. "Think I can have some alcohol in it?"

"Sure. I have a flask of vodka in my purse."

Raina gave her grandma a peck on the cheek. "Love you."

Po Po handed her a ten. "Why don't I go buy some formula and a bottle while you wait in the Starbucks line with the baby? I'd take the baby with me, except"—she lowered her voice to a whisper—"it's dangerous where I'm going."

"Um, sure." The baby had fallen asleep by this time.

A few minutes later, Raina sipped an iced caramel macchiato at a small table. The baby still slept blissfully in her arm. The Saturday morning shoppers barely spared a glance at the two. Anonymity was a wonderful thing.

She tried the number in the diaper bag again, leaving another message and her grandma's cell number.

"Let's go. We need to get out of here. Now!" Po Po said when she came back. "We'll call Matthew to come get the baby at your place once we're on the road."

"Matthew might be on his way already. He's not going to be happy if we send him on a wild goose chase. And it's raining like crazy. We shouldn't take the baby outside."

Po Po glanced behind her. Her knuckles whitened around the handle of the plastic bags she carried.

Raina followed her grandma's gaze. Two men shouted at each other by the clothes department. A store associate tried to calm the men down. The taller man pointed at Po Po and spoke animatedly. The three of them started walking toward Starbucks.

"Yo! Old Chinese woman. Where's my Jiggle Me doll?" the taller man shouted.

"It's the only one left in the area," said the shorter man. "And it's mine. I called the store to have them put it on hold for me."

A woman stopped in her tracks. She turned to study Po Po. "How much do you want for the Jiggle Me doll?" She whipped out a fifty-dollar bill from her purse. "I must have it for my daughter."

The cell phone in Raina's hands vibrated. She glanced at the new text message.

Meet me outside old bookstore. Parking Bullseye nightmare. Have info on Sui Yuk.

Raina stood, swinging the diaper bag onto her shoulder. The men looked ready to wrestle her grandma. "Let's roll."

The taller man broke away and ran toward Po Po. "Stop."

"It's mine!" The shorter man grabbed the

back of the taller man's jacket and yanked him up short. They grappled, and the two fell to the ground.

The woman pulled out another fifty. She shoved the money in Po Po's face and grabbed the shopping bags. "Here. Let me have the doll."

Po Po slapped away the woman's hand. Raina and her grandma rushed out of the store to the sound of pounding footsteps and strains of "Grandma Got Run Over by a Reindeer."

2

LET'S DANCE

Raina unlocked her faded red Honda, and they piled in. She handed the baby to her grandma and started the engine.

Po Po pulled a blanket out of the diaper bag and swaddled the child. "Where are we going?"

"The other side of the shopping plaza," Raina said as she backed out of her parking spot. "I got a text from someone who claims to have info on Sui Yuk Liang."

"At the empty storefront? What about the police?"

"It's not like we're running off with the baby. We're just following up on a lead while it's still hot."

"If you think about it, we're actually saving him," Po Po said. "If we'd stayed, he might get trampled at the store. And we could always go back once things die down at Bullseye."

Raina gave Po Po a sideways glance. Her grandma's logic was unconventional at best, but downright dubious when she fished for excitement. Was this what she had to look forward to when she turned seventy-five? She parked and reached for the baby. "Can you send Matthew a text to let him know we're here? I'm going outside with the baby."

She got out, juggling the diaper bag and the baby. There was no sign of Sui Yuk Liang. The baby grabbed a strand of her curly black hair and stuffed it into his mouth, drooling all over her shoulder in the process. "Good thing you're a cutie."

The mega bookstore had left a year ago, but the town hadn't been able to lure another big box store into the retail space. The windows of the empty building gaped at the shoppers across the parking lot like a toothless crone.

Raina took shelter under the overhanging canopy. Her curly hair responded to the drizzle like an angry cat, spreading itself like a wild halo around her head. Asian Carrot Top on the go. This was the reason she didn't date much in the winter.

"Psst. Over here," a voice said over her left shoulder.

Raina swung around and frowned at the man hidden in the shadow of the building. He beckoned for her to come closer even as he crossed the space between them. The man appeared to be in his early fifties with a touch of gray in his brown hair that would have been distinguished on anyone else. But his squinty brown eyes made the hair on the back of Raina's neck stand to attention. She tightened her grip on the baby as she sneaked a glance at her car.

"Aaron Wheeler, madam," the man said, holding out a hand. The wind shifted and the acrid stench of cigarettes from his worn parka wafted like a dust cloud around her.

She gave him a fake apologetic smile, but she was secretly glad she could use the baby and diaper bag as an excuse not to shake Aaron's hand. "I've already called the police. They are on their way."

"Oh, there is no need for that. I'm here to pick up my son. The wife probably forgot her medication. It's postpartum depression." He sighed with a weariness that irritated Raina, as if he were a saint for putting up with his wife. "I'll strap junior in his car seat and take a drive to see if I can find Sui Yuk. It's the second time she's wandered off this month."

Raina patted the baby's small back and studied Aaron. He looked old enough to be Sui Yuk's father rather than the baby's. Sure, there were December-May relationships, but the child didn't look bi-racial. "Where is his birthmark located?"

Aaron stiffened as if he were offended. "What is this? A test?"

"Why isn't Sui Yuk here with you?"

"Not that it's any of your business, but she's having a hard time adjusting to mother-hood. She wanders off sometimes." He stepped closer, looming over her. His face tensed and his eyes tightened into a scowl. "The baby is mine. I'm not wading though bureaucratic red tape to get him back."

Raina straightened, hoping her five feet three inches appeared to take up physical space like a puffed-up angry cat. Her heart raced at the veiled threat, but she wasn't going to let him see her fear. "You need to talk to social services or the police. I called the number in the diaper bag because I hoped whoever answered would tell Sui Yuk to contact me."

He took a deep breath, visibly forcing himself to relax. "Can I hold him? I haven't seen my baby in a couple of days. The ex wouldn't let me see him as much as I would like."

"How did you get divorced in the last five minutes?"

"What?"

"I said—"

"Just give me the baby," he said through gritted teeth.

Raina held the baby closer against her chest. Despite the cold, a bead of sweat rolled down the small of her back. A car rumbled past, blaring a few strands of "Rudolph the Red-Nosed Reindeer." She swallowed the knot in her throat and opened her mouth. "When you can prove—"

His hand snaked out, grabbing a corner of the blanket.

Raina twisted, using her body as a shield. "Stop it. You're going to make me drop him." She tightened her grip on the baby. He squirmed and let out a cry.

Aaron tugged at the blanket until a chubby leg was exposed. He grabbed the leg and pulled. The child's cry grew more piercing.

She clawed at his hands with her nails. "You're hurting him!"

His arm curled around her waist, but he didn't let go. "He's mine!"

"What is going on here?" called Po Po from behind her.

Raina's heart stopped at the thought of Aaron knocking over her seventy-five-year-old grandma. She opened her mouth and screamed. A blood-curdling sound that matched the infant's cry.

Po Po swung her beach bag-sized purse and smacked it against Aaron's head. Pain spread across his face and he spun around. "What the—"

Raina staggered backward. Her gaze scanned the area, looking for a safe place to set the baby. She wedged the child in the space between the communal mailbox and the empty building. The mailbox should prevent anyone from accidentally stepping on him.

As Aaron advanced toward her, Po Po stepped back, clutching her purse.

His fingers curled into fists. "Listen, you old bat—"

Po Po whipped out her pepper spray and blasted him.

Aaron jerked and covered his face with his hands. He screamed like a girly man.

Raina smacked him with the diaper bag. It ricocheted off his shoulders and smashed onto her nose. She yelped in pain and stumbled against Aaron, knocking both of them onto the wet concrete sidewalk.

As he picked himself up, her grandma slapped him with her purse. She sprayed him again. Another quick blast that even made Raina's eyes sting. "Come on, baby, let's dance."

He hunched his shoulders and fumbled sideways, almost falling again in his haste to leave. "Keep the baby! The money isn't worth this."

Po Po swung her purse above her head and threw it against his back. He yelped, grabbed his back, and scrambled away.

Raina's jaw dropped. Forget flies. She could catch hummingbirds with her mouth. She turned her head slowly to stare at her grandma. What was that? She'd always known Po Po to be a fighter, but she'd never thought it was literal.

Po Po held out her hand for a high five. "Show me some love."

Raina patted her grandma's hand dutifully. Her heart was still participating in a race she didn't want to be in.

Po Po was literally bouncing from the adrenaline. "Where's the baby?"

Raina rushed to the mailbox, fearing the worst, but the baby sucked his finger as he stared at a spider wrapping his lunch. She scooped the child into her arms and inspected his leg. It was slightly red around the ankle, but there was no bruise. She rubbed it gently. "Poor baby," she murmured.

"Is the little guy okay?" Po Po asked.

Raina nodded. "Where are the police? I thought you said they were on their way."

Po Po shrugged. "Let's go to your apartment. He might show up with friends next time."

After they piled into her car, Raina hit the locks. It took her two tries to insert the key in the ignition. By the time she pulled out from the driveway, the familiar citrus air freshener and the warmth from the heater helped slow her heart rate. After several rattled breaths, the jittery feeling disappeared.

Raina drove as if she had a car full of eggs. She hoped the one time she drove a child around without a car seat wouldn't be the first time she got a ticket. The other drivers must have thought they were sharing the road with a new student driver. The baby slept in Po Po's arms without a care in the world.

The earlier drizzle became a downpour as

if a water tower were cracked in half. The twinkling Christmas lights and large wreaths adorning the lampposts in the downtown area became a blur.

"Please call Matthew to let him know that we are heading back to my apartment with the baby," Raina said.

She hoped she wouldn't get in trouble for leaving, but what choice did she have? If they had stayed outside the store, the three of them would be soaked and Aaron might return. Neither was returning to Bullseye an option. There was no telling if the other shoppers would continue to harass them over the Jiggle Me doll.

Instead of calling Matthew, Po Po called Donna, the front desk clerk who also worked as the dispatcher. It looked like her grandma wasn't too keen on facing his annoyance either.

Did she make the right decision by calling Aaron Wheeler? Was she overanalyzing this? Sure, Sui Yuk Liang could have put the baby on top of the diaper bag in the restroom. But the floors were disgusting when Raina had used the restroom prior to her encounter with the young mom. Crumpled paper towels and unidentifiable wet spots on the floors. Yuck. Management should have increased the cleaning schedule with so many shoppers in the store.

She pulled into the parking lot at the back of her small apartment complex. The eight units were divided into two strips and faced one another over a courtyard like the green houses on a Monopoly game.

"When are the police going to get here?" Raina asked as she opened the front door.

She grimaced at the soreness in her shoulder as she dropped the three-ton diaper bag on the living room floor. And here she thought her grandma's beach bag-size purse was a pain to lug around. As she turned on the lamp next to the new-to-me sofa, she rubbed her aching shoulder.

"Maybe another hour? Donna said

things"—Po Po averted her gaze—"got out of hand after we left the store. Matthew and Officer Hopper are busy taking statements right now."

Oh great. They were going to be in an awesome mood when they finally showed up. "What happened?"

"The usual Christmas stuff. A shoving match. A broken window. Oh, a riot that shut down the store for the day."

"We're in deep sh—"

"Language, Rainy. Little ears are listening." Po Po glanced at the infant in her arms. "There's no proof the riot has anything to do with us."

Raina looked pointedly at the Jiggle Me doll sticking out of the plastic bag next to the diaper bag.

"Finders keepers. Whiners weepers. It wasn't my fault the two men would rather argue with each other than hustle to the checkout line. I paid for it. It's mine," Po Po said. "Anywho, I can't wait to see Lila's face when she opens her present. I'm winning the best great-gran award."

Raina sighed and dropped the subject. She didn't want to lose the chance to put her name on the gift tag. Mercenary? Yes, but it was for a good cause. She needed to get back into the rest of the family's good graces without seeming like she was groveling.

Life was sure more exciting with her grandma around. Her growling stomach told her it was late afternoon. A quick glance at the clock with gilded koi fishes swimming around the dial confirmed what her body already knew. Two o'clock. Time to wolf down some food before the cops got here.

Po Po held out the baby. "Why don't I get the mail for you?"

For a moment, Raina experienced a sense of déjà vu. It was like her morning with Sui Yuk all over again. She grabbed the child. "The mail can wait. We should eat before the cops get here."

Po Po snatched the keys from the narrow

table next to her front door. "No, I insist. I want to see the ads for this week. Only a few more shopping days left before Christmas."

"Don't you want to leave your purse—"

Her grandma hustled out of the apartment as if she were using a "get out of jail free" card.

The baby's face scrunched up and his little arms windmilled. Her niece Lila had the same expression right before she exploded into her diaper. No wonder her grandma was hiding out until the cleanup was done.

Raina gently placed the baby on the beige carpet. He was still young enough that she didn't have to worry about him rolling anywhere. She headed to her shoebox of a kitchen for another cup of coffee to give the baby time to finish his business. The scent of brewing coffee almost masked the smell of poo filling the small apartment. The knot between her shoulder blades loosened as the tension oozed out of her body.

Everything turned out okay. The police

would pick up the baby, and being stood up was the perfect excuse to ward off any future duties with the foreign exchange student. Life was good.

After a quick diaper change, Raina was cooing to the baby when her grandma returned with the mail. "Aaron said the baby is his."

They both stared at the almond-shaped brown eyes and downy black hair on the baby.

"Adoption?" Po Po said doubtfully. "But that wouldn't explain Sui Yuk Liang. Why do you think he wants the baby?"

"Your guess is as good as mine. Do you think we should do a reverse lookup on the phone number in the diaper bag?"

"It's not a bad idea. That way we would at least know which part of town to avoid until this dies down."

"Isn't it odd Aaron mentioned money? Do you think he's being paid to retrieve the child?"

"For who? Sui Yuk?"

"Now that is the million-dollar question."

Knock! Knock!

Raina's pulse jumped. She wasn't sure how much more excitement she could take. Today was supposed to be a mundane Saturday morning. Aaron couldn't have followed her home.

She squinted in her peephole. E. Matthew Louie. Her breath rushed out in relief. The police finally arrived. As usual, her ex-boyfriend always managed to show up after the action was over.

3

BRINGING SEXY BACK

Droplets of rain clung to Matthew's black hair. His navy-blue sweater looked damp, as if he hadn't bothered with an umbrella for the short distance from his police cruiser to her apartment. The warmth radiated off him, raising the humidity in the space between them. His body always ran warmer than hers—the perfect bedmate for a long winter night.

Matthew leaned down as if to kiss her. "Hi, Rainy."

Raina inhaled his citrus and sage scent,

but shifted so his lips grazed her cheek. "Boy, am I glad to see you." She stepped aside so he could come in.

He smiled as if he heard an offer he couldn't resist. When he saw Po Po sitting on the sofa with the baby, he straightened. His gold-flecked brown eyes lost their come-hither sultry gaze.

"So you're bringing sexy back, huh?" Po Po asked.

He flushed as if he were caught with his hands in the honey pot. "No, madam."

"I wouldn't want to see my Rainy upset again."

Raina held up her hands. "Whoa! I'm not—"

"Of course not. I wouldn't want to see her upset either," he said.

"She tells me it's over. I'm assuming you're not one of those stalker types," Po Po continued, ignoring Raina.

Matthew winced. "Yes. I mean no. I'm not a stalker."

Raina glanced down to hide her grin. A flustered Matthew was a rare sight. His grandma, Maggie Louie, and Po Po had been best friends for the last fifty-five years. Po Po had been like another grandparent to him, just as Maggie Louie had been to Raina. But there was no hint of this now. Po Po was a mother bear protecting her cub.

"Several officers are at Bullseye doing crowd control and taking statements," Matthew said. "It's the reason I'm here instead of an officer."

Raina stared at the koi clock above her TV. She bit her lip to hide her smile. Even flustered, Matthew handled her grandma like an old pro.

Po Po stood with the baby. "Boy, do I need a nap. Wake me up when it's my turn." She went into the bedroom and closed the door.

Matthew sighed. "Is there any way you could control her?"

"With what? A tranquilizer dart in her butt?"

"You'll need a dose that could drop an elephant," he mumbled, pulling a notebook from his back pocket. "Tell me what happened."

Raina told him everything that happened after Sui Yuk's disappearance from Bullseye. He made notes and asked her the same questions in several creative ways as if to trip her up. "What happens now?"

"I need to get Wong Po Po's statement," he said, flipping to a blank page on his notebook.

"No. I mean what happens after this?"

"The social worker picks up the baby. And we'll try to find the mother and Aaron Wheeler."

"Oh, I don't get to keep the baby for a bit?"

He narrowed his eyes as if studying her. "Is your biological clock speeding up?"

Raina flushed but lifted her chin. "Those are fighting words. They sound as bad as asking if I'm on my period. But I'm going to be the bigger person here and ignore them."

"Why would you want a baby hanging around here?"

"Why not? It's Christmas—the season to apply for sainthood. I feel a certain responsibility toward the little guy."

"Ah," he said. "Your mother's Chinese superstition."

Raina stiffened and gave him the evil eye. He was probably right. Her mom's teachings came out at the oddest moments. It was strange how her grandma embraced all things American while her mom seemed to continually search for her roots.

"You really don't want to get involved in this. Sometimes we find the mother, and sometimes we don't. I know you're looking for a project to get over us, but this is not it."

"I'm surprise your head doesn't pop off at times. Not everything is about you." Raina grabbed the diaper bag and stalked into her bedroom.

Po Po handed her the baby. "Are you okay?"

"I'm fine. It's your turn," Raina said.

Po Po opened her mouth but changed her

mind and left, closing the bedroom door behind her.

Raina cuddled the soft body close. All milk and innocence. The baby's little hand grabbed a strand of her hair and stuffed it into his mouth. She was a sucker for round chubby cheeks and crankles.

They needed to give the child a temporary name. It was awkward using baby or infant when addressing him. Maybe Baby Liang. Or BL. She shook her head. No, naming him would be like feeding a stray kitten. Once she named him, he'd keep reappearing in her life.

She checked his diaper, but he was still dry. He gave her a gummy smile, drool trickling off the side of his mouth. She wiped it with her finger and wiped it on her shirt.

With BL resting on her shoulders, she went back to the living room and handed him to her grandma. Po Po was in the middle of describing her fight with her hand poised in front of Matthew as if she were about to blast him with an imaginary pepper spray.

"Sorry for interrupting, but does anyone want any Ramen?" Raina asked. "I haven't had lunch yet."

Po Po made a face and shook her head. Matthew also declined.

Raina shrugged. More food for her. These two would come sniffing around like stray cats once she got around to filling her pantry. While she waited for the water to boil, she made up a bottle of formula and handed it to her grandma. On the way back into the kitchen, she grabbed her cell phone.

It powered on and the screen lit up. Woo-hoo! She found the recent call list and studied Aaron's phone number. It looked familiar, but she couldn't place where she'd seen it before. A few minutes later she was on her Goodwill dining room table, slurping noodles and searching for a reverse phone number site on her laptop.

Matthew finished up his statement with Po Po and joined her. He turned a chair around and straddled it. "Still not touching the inheritance from your grandfather?"

Raina shook her head. "He wanted to use the money to support his other family in China. Until I figure out if I want to honor his wishes, the money is off-limits."

"At least your cousins are no longer contesting the will. What are their opinions of the situation?"

Raina glanced at the living room. Her grandma bounced BL on her lap, cooing at him as if he were one of her grandsons. "Po Po wants to keep Ah Gong's disgrace from the rest of the family a little longer."

"But that's not fair to you. Everyone thinks you influenced your granddad to disinherit them."

Raina shrugged with a nonchalance she didn't feel. As long as her grandma wasn't weeping from the discovery that her marriage was a sham, what did it matter how her cousins treated her? "They'll apologize when they find out."

Matthew gave her a doubtful look but smiled to lighten the mood. "A lot of women would be embarrassed to be chowing noodles like this in front of a man."

Raina attempted to roll her eyes at his bantering to show her appreciation, but only managed to blink instead. "We've known each other too long for me to care. Besides, we're not together anymore. You should be happy I'm not picking my nose."

"Now that's an attractive image."

Raina swiped at the soup dripping down her chin with the back of her hand. "I'm glad you approve. You treat your buddies better than you do your girlfriend." Too bad it took her ten years to figure this out.

"I spent a month tracking down used car parts for your totaled car. I wouldn't do that for a friend."

Her father had taught her how to drive in the old Honda Accord. It was the only thing she'd inherited from him. Matthew was one of the few people who knew how much the car meant to her. "You just wanted to get in my pants again."

"You're giving me a bad rep here. After all I've done, that's my agenda, huh?"

It might not be his agenda, but he was going to take a shot at it anyway. Typical.

She typed in Aaron's phone number on the search bar. Not that she was bored with their conversation, but the comfortable familiarity made her heart ache. This was what happened when she'd spent her entire life chasing a man who didn't want to be caught.

"Rainy?"

She glanced at Matthew. "Sorry, what did you say?"

"I'm your knight in shining armor. Don't I deserve a kiss for fixing your car?"

"I would rather pick your belly lint. I made you dinner. We're squared."

Matthew threw back his head and laughed. "This is why I love you."

Raina ignored his comment. She already knew he loved her. That wasn't their problem.

"Sui Yuk Liang had to be desperate if she was willing to leave her baby with a stranger."

"You are over thinking this. Doesn't postpartum depression make women do crazy things like howl at the moon?"

"You really don't know anything about pregnancy or babies, do you?"

"So, I'm a man."

She sat back in her chair and studied him. "But don't you want a baby and wife someday?"

He stared back into the living room where Po Po was now singing a Chinese lullaby to the child. The koi clock ticked, filling the silence between them. Raina held her breath, knowing what the answer would be, but hoping all the same.

After what seemed like an eternity, he glanced back at her. "No."

His parents' marriage was a series of slammed doors and fists on soft flesh. When his father finally left, his mother only hung around long enough to make sure her mom would take Matthew in. And then one day, poof, she was gone too. Though Matthew might love Raina in the best way he knew how, it wasn't enough anymore.

She swallowed her disappointment. "Then stop bringing sexy back. If you care for me, you should let me go."

"Sorry. This is the first time we have spoken in months. I thought we were at the friends' stage by now."

Right. As if he flirted this outrageously with his buddies. "I'm not there yet. I need more space."

"How about dinner tomorrow night? Entirely platonic. Just friends hanging out."

"Changing subjects. Do you think Aaron had anything to do with Sui Yuk's disappearance?"

He shook his head. "It's probably the hormones."

She gave him a disgusted look. "At least you're not blaming her disappearance on PMS."

"There's no winning no matter what I say. I can't launch an investigation on nothing more substantial than your suspicion. She hasn't even disappeared for more than twenty-four hours. For all we know, she could report a kidnapping later. Why don't you just wait and see what turns up? I'll run her name through the databases when I get a chance. Besides, I have more urgent cases on my desk right at the moment."

Raina blushed. Of course he had other important cases. He was a grown-up with a career job while she was floundering as a pretend graduate student after giving up her promising career as a civil engineer.

She glanced at the laptop screen and her eyes widened. She gasped and sucked soup down the wrong pipe. Her eyes filled up with tears, and she couldn't stop coughing. Matthew rushed around the table and patted her on the back.

"Are you okay, Rainy?" Po Po called out from the living room.

Raina waved and whispered, "Fine. I'm fine." When she finally was able to talk without coughing, she pointed at her laptop screen. "Aaron called from the Gold Springs Birth Resort."

Matthew glanced at the laptop and then back at her. "Didn't I tell you to leave the detective work to me?"

Po Po rushed into the dining nook with the baby. "I don't like the idea of you working at the resort with Aaron hanging around there."

Matthew glanced from her grandma to Raina, understanding spread across his face. "No. No. You're going to quit this job and find something else. There are plenty of places looking for holiday help."

Raina stiffened at the tone of his voice. "Are you going to pay my bills?" She paused as if waiting for an answer. "I didn't think so."

He clenched his jaw as if realizing he'd taken the wrong tactic with her.

"That was the perfect thing to say to

Rainy," Po Po said. "Since you're neither her boyfriend nor her husband."

He held up both hands as if he were surrendering. "I'm just worried."

"Your concern is noted," Raina said through clenched teeth, "but I'm filling in for my friend Sonia. If I just bail, it'd jeopardize her job." Did Matthew think he had a right to boss her around?

She had no intention of wrangling with Aaron again, at least not without her grandma at her side. If Aaron worked at the resort, he might have met Sui Yuk Liang there.

Raina should sneak a peek at the guest list tomorrow. Was Sui Yuk dealing with postpartum depression and forgot her baby? If this was the case, Raina had to at least let her know the social worker took temporary custody of BL. "Don't worry. I'll have pepper spray in my pocket the entire time."

4

MONEY, COME AWAY

The next morning, Raina rose when the sky was still a deep purple for her run. According to the forecast, today would be her last run for a few days before even heavier rainstorms moved into the area. She dressed in layers and set off for Hook Park, running around Mildred's Pond and the winding path up to the highest point in the park.

She'd tossed and turned the entire night. It didn't help that BL's baby powder scent still clung to her sheets. She'd saved the baby yesterday from Aaron Wheeler. According to an old Chinese superstition, by changing his fate, she was now responsible for BL. Not that she was superstitious. Besides, BL was either with a foster family or with his mother and well beyond her reach. She'd done her duty, and his ancestors would have no reason to be upset with her.

Her best friend, Eden Small, would laugh if she knew what Raina was thinking. The hard-nosed reporter was out of town visiting family in Southern California. She'd left with the admonition to call if anything interesting were to happen. As the new Assistant Chief-in-Editor, Eden was on a mission to prove she could run the town's newspaper. But interesting was relative.

When Raina got home, she quickly showered and changed into the resort's standard-issue black shirt with the baby bump logo. She was making her second cup of hazelnut coffee when the phone rang.

"Hi, is this Raina Sun?" said the unfamiliar voice. The voice was warm and relaxed, like sipping an iced mai tai under an umbrella.

The phone number on caller ID wasn't one she recognized, and she doubted Aaron Wheeler could change his voice. "Yes?"

"Erm, your uncle gave me your phone number. He said you could show me a good time."

"What?"

"No, no. Please don't hang up." He sounded panicked. "Sorry, that didn't come out right. I'm not implying that you're a..."

Raina smiled in amusement. Normally she wouldn't linger on the phone with a stranger, but she'd vowed to welcome new experiences into her life. She had to get over Matthew even if it killed her. "Which one?"

He cleared his throat. "Maybe a fancy one that a guy can take to a wedding?"

She imagined him tugging at the collar of his shirt. After yesterday, this bizarre conversation was fun. "I meant which uncle. I have six of them."

"Oh." He was silent for a heartbeat. "I should go."

"No, no—"

The line went dead. First Sui Yuk handed her a baby, next Aaron Wheeler tried to snatch BL away. And now this. Who said there wasn't life after Matthew?

It wasn't lost on her that she put her life into two categories—Before Matthew and After Matthew. She needed to take up knitting or something. Her nightly dates with Ben and Jerry weren't doing much for her waistline. Their repeated litany to eat them kept her mood swinging from guilt to pleasure too many times a night for her comfort.

During the short drive to the Gold Country Birth Resort, Raina kept glancing at her rearview mirror, expecting Aaron Wheeler to pop up. Her shoulders were tensed by the time she parked her car behind the large community room. The man didn't intimidate her, but she slipped her pepper spray into her pockets before getting out of the car, just in case.

Raina hunched her shoulders against the chill and jogged to the large utility room. The room housed commercial washers and dryers, a small table, and two mismatched chairs. The radio on the table blared Spanish music as if it were in a room full of senior citizens with dead batteries in their hearing aids.

Lucille, a motherly looking Mexican woman in her mid-thirties, folded and stacked clean towels into the maid's cart. She turned down the radio, and they exchanged greetings. Raina grabbed a towel and began folding it.

"It's nice of you to fill in for Sonia," Lucille said, wiggling the cigarette in the corner of her mouth. "But Mexico isn't much of a honeymoon if you want my opinion. I would go to Hawaii. White sandy beaches and a cabana boy in a Speedo. Now that would be a honeymoon."

"It's not a problem. I need the money. How was Sonia supposed to have a honeymoon with her husband if there was a cabana boy hanging around?"

"Send the husband to pick up tampons at the convenience store."

Raina laughed to show she got the joke. They worked quietly for a couple of minutes, before she casually asked, "Is there an Aaron Wheeler on the staff?"

"The name doesn't sound familiar."

"He's about five foot ten and fifties with gray in his brown hair. And his teeth are yellowed from smoking."

Lucille gave Raina a sharp look. "I hope you're not going to give me a lecture on how smoking is going to kill me. You have that scrawny look that tells me you're a health nut."

Raina shook her head. "I'm not a health nut. I'm only skinny because I don't have money to buy good food." Which wasn't strictly true.

Lucille chuckled. "As long as you pull your own weight when we clean, I don't care if you're a wet noodle."

Once the cart was loaded, Lucille pulled out a list from her pocket and studied it. "We are cleaning the bungalows on the southern end of the property today."

Raina eyed the guest list. Would it look suspicious if she asked to take a look at it? Guests normally ignored the housekeeping staff as if they were part of the furniture. Lucille might know the goings-on at the resort, but how to bring up Sui Yuk Liang without looking like Raina was fishing?

Lucille stuffed the list back into her pocket. "Let's hope the guests are busy eating lunch at the community rooms. I hate it when they sit in the rooms, watching me like I'm a freak show."

"I thought we were invisible to hotel guests."

"It's a different clientele here."

"Paranoid, maybe?"

Lucille shrugged her amply padded shoulders. "Pregnancy makes some women crazy."

"What is a birth resort? Is it like a spa resort catering to pregnant women?"

"Foreign pregnant women. Sometimes they have someone with them to take care of them during their stay. Like a family member or a personal maid."

"What—"

Lucille knocked on Suite Fifteen's door. "Housekeeping!"

The individual one- or two-bedroom bungalow suites were scattered among the landscaped trees. There was just enough breathing room to make Raina feel like the guests were staying in the granny flat of a friend.

Soon the two of them settled into a rhythm. Lucille would gather the dirty sheets while Raina put on clean ones. They alternated turns at cleaning the kitchenette and the bathroom.

Raina picked up where they had left off

earlier. "Do the guests stay until they give birth?"

"Smart girl."

"And they return to their countries after labor and delivery," Raina said, thinking out loud. If they had stayed, Eden would have sniffed this story out. As it was, these guests were like other foreign tourists in the country for an extended stay.

Lucille nodded. "These aren't anchor babies."

Raina frowned. The only advantage to giving birth in the U.S. was the automatic citizenship granted to the child. Why go through all this trouble if the women return home with their babies? She'd always taken her citizenship for granted, sometimes even with annoyance when the jury duty notice showed up in the mail.

The door opened and an overpowering rose scent filled the room. Raina's eyes watered as her seasonal allergies went haywire from the perfume. By the time the resort owner came into view, Raina was wiping her nose on the sleeve of her shirt.

Cecelia Wagner was in her late forties with manly features—a hawk nose and square chin—that gave an overall impression of vigorous health. Her waist-length mousy brown hair was streaked with gray. She had once told Raina she got tired of dying it since her money was more attractive to men than her hair.

She waved to get their attention as if her perfume hadn't already stopped all activity in the room. "Sorry for interrupting. Lucille, could you please pack up the guest's things in Suite Eighteen? She was supposed to check out two days ago. Since she hadn't told me otherwise, I'm assuming she didn't want her things."

"How long are we going to keep the things this time?" Lucille glanced at Raina. "Some of our guests spend their entire stay shopping. And because of the weight limitations on baggage, they leave a lot of it behind." Her nostrils flared as if she smelled something rotten. "With all that money to burn, you would think they could tip the help better," she muttered under her breath.

Raina ignored the extra comment. "Have they ever asked for us to ship it to them? I know the guests are wealthy in their own countries, but this seems like a waste."

"Tell me about it. They take home the good stuff, but the things from Bullseye just aren't good enough. Housekeeping gets first dibs on them after the thirty-day holding period." Lucille eyed her slyly. "Well, I get first dibs. You being a temp and all."

"Of course," Raina said placidly. She doubted there would be anything she would want from a pregnant woman. "Who's the guest in Suite Eight—"

A cell phone rang. *Money, come away / Get in my pocket, here to stay...*

Cecelia grabbed the cell phone clipped to her elastic waistband. "Hello, this is Cecelia Wagner." As she listened, her eyes grew wider. "Officer, am I in trouble? Do I need a lawyer?"

Raina paused in the act of tucking in the corner of the sheet. Either Cecelia was being sued or she was needed at the police station. Did the police also run a reverse lookup on the number in the diaper bag and connect it to the resort? What she wouldn't give to have said yes to breakfast with Matthew to pick his brain on the Sui Yuk Liang disappearance case.

"I can't go to the station right now. It's the middle of the day. I have a business to run," Cecelia said into the phone. She listened. "Alright, I'll be there in half an hour." She disconnected the call and stared at the phone for several heartbeats.

Raina cleared her throat, hoping she looked concerned rather than nosy. "Cecelia, is everything okay?"

The resort owner ignored her.

Raina glanced at Lucille, who shrugged at her. "Cecelia, are—"

Cecelia shoved her phone back into the clip at her waistband. "Yes...fine." She left the room without further ado.

"What you think that is about?" Raina asked.

Lucille immediately opened the patio door and an inviting breeze swept into the room, cleaning the air. "Who knows? Someone should tell her that less is more. You shouldn't smell someone before you see them."

Raina sneezed. *So said the pot calling the kettle black.* The cigarette smoke rolling off Lucille could cure a ham. "Who is the guest in Suite Eighteen?"

Lucille pulled out her guest list. "Some lady called Sui Yuk Liang. Ah, the one that was busy making cow eyes at Eric, Cecelia's ex-husband, and Scotty, the pool boy." She gave Raina a sly look. "Who is also Cecelia's new boy toy."

Bingo! Raina cleared her throat to give

herself time to calm down. "Cecelia's ex-husband works here?"

"Oh yeah. He's the head landscaper. If you haven't noticed, Cecelia likes to keep her men on a short leash."

"I don't understand. She's not exactly"—Raina grimaced—"a sexpot."

"Money, kiddo. That's the way the world works. And Cecelia has far more of it than either man."

Raina wiped the small tabletop next to the television cabinet. *Play it cool*, said a small voice inside her head. "This guest poached on both of Cecelia's men while she was pregnant? I'm assuming she's not pregnant anymore."

Lucille grabbed the handle of the maid's cart. "Ready to go?"

Raina held the door opened. "Yes."

"Now here's an unexplained miracle," Lucille continued as they headed toward the next bungalow. "Sui Yuk went into labor and had a stillbirth at the hospital. She came back a month later with a baby boy."

5

DRAMA QUEEN

After making her strange comment, Lucille clammed up. She would talk, but it wasn't anything of real interest. Raina tried asking questions about Sui Yuk Liang in a roundabout way, but no dice.

Raina didn't know what to make of Lucille's statement about BL. How could there be a mistake about the stillbirth? This wasn't one of those situations where there could be a gray area. Wouldn't there be witnesses like a doctor and nurses?

If there was a stillbirth, then BL couldn't be Sui Yuk's baby. Were BL's parents out there searching for him? Poor little guy.

The next three hours flew by in a blur. Raina wanted to rush into Suite Eighteen to make a sweep of the room. Surprisingly, Lucille was meticulous when it came to her job, checking each suite off her list in numeric order. It took all of Raina's willpower to hold her impatience in check.

When Lucille took a smoking break, Raina texted Matthew, asking if he was available for dinner. Now that she had more information about Sui Yuk Liang, she wanted to see what turned up when he ran the missing mom's name through the police databases. A few seconds later, her cell phone dinged. She clicked on his reply.

NO CAN DO. GOT A HIT AND RUN.

Raina suppressed her flash of disappointment. She didn't need his help. It wasn't like finding a missing person was rocket science. How hard could it be to post up a couple of flyers and call around at the local hospitals?

Lucille came back, and they moved to Suite Eighteen. Hallelujah!

The sun didn't make an appearance the entire day. The low outdoor lights lit the meandering pathways on the property. If Raina squinted hard enough, she could pretend the women she passed were everyday tourists. Except the silhouette of their bulging stomachs told a different story.

The women sat on the park benches or on their lounge chairs in the small patio next to the front door of their bungalows. It was nippy outside, but it was probably better than being cooped up inside their rooms day after day. And Lucille was right. While the women had a stillness about them as if they were listening to something internal, their eyes watched everything with distrust. It fairly made Raina's skin crawl because they belonged to a world in which she had no idea how to navigate. But boy, she'd love to have one of them give her the skinny on Sui Yuk Liang.

They stopped to grab some boxes from a nearby utility closet. Suite Eighteen was mind numbingly similar to all the other rooms she'd cleaned. The large main room included the living room, dining nook, and kitchenette. The front room alone was bigger than Raina's apartment.

Lucille made a beeline for the laptop on the sofa. "This would make a great Christmas present for my son. Right now he has to type his papers at the library or the computer labs at the high school."

Raina opened and closed the kitchen cabinets. Other than several packages of saltine crackers and a box of cereal, there wasn't much else in the kitchen. Even the trashcan was empty. "I thought you said we have to hold the discarded things for thirty days. Christmas is only six days from now. Besides, the laptop is from China. Is the keyboard even the same as the one we use here?"

There was a setting to reprogram the keyboard layout so the laptop could be used in the United States. However, Lucille didn't need to know this. Raina didn't want her co-worker to take the laptop home before she got a chance to search through the files.

This almost felt like lost relatives coming to claim a part of an estate before the dead person was even properly buried. It left a bad taste in her mouth.

Lucille opened the laptop and her smile disappeared. "There's alphabets, but there's other things on the keys too."

Raina walked over to the sofa and peeked over Lucille's shoulder. "Those are the keystrokes for typing Chinese characters if the user doesn't want to use the Pinyin system of writing."

Lucille closed the laptop, and tossed it back on the sofa. "I should have lined up at

Best Buy on Black Friday," she muttered under her breath.

"But then you would have missed Thanksgiving with your family."

Lucille shrugged. "Some things are more important than food."

Raina kept silent and moved into the bedroom. A high-thread-count floral sheet set covered the bed. Apparently Sui Yuk Liang traveled with her own sheets. Clothes still hung on the rack in the closet, makeup on the vanity, and the empty suitcases waiting to be filled in the corner. The crib still had diapers stacked next to it on the floor.

Warning bells clamored in Raina's mind. She went back into the living room. "Are you sure the guest checked out? Her makeup is still here."

Lucille tapped on her cell phone with a goofy smile on her face. She looked up at Raina's entrance. "You can call Cecelia to straighten it out." She stood, patting her hair and smoothing her shirt. "I'm taking a smoking break. Be back in a few minutes."

"Wait! I thought Cecelia left for the police station."

Lucille hurried toward the door, calling over her shoulder, "Just freshen up the room then. We can always deal with packing up the stuff tomorrow."

After Lucille left, Raina powered on the laptop. While she waited for it to boot up, she picked up the nearby trashcan and peered inside. The crumbled sheet of paper between a plastic cup and a leaking take-out carton with pungent leftovers caught her attention. She pinched the paper between her thumb and index finger and pulled it out. Droplets of a creamy sauce from the take-out carton splattered on her hand. She grimaced in distaste, but pulled out the paper and unfolded it.

L AST WARNING. G IVE ME BACK MY BABY.

The handwriting, all sharp curves and

slashes, sent a chill down her spine. There was no longer any doubt that Sui Yuk Liang gave the baby to Raina for safekeeping. She snapped a photo of the threatening note with her cell phone and sent it off to Matthew with a text to let him know she was keeping the original.

This couldn't be the first time Sui Yuk had received a threatening note. If it were the first, wouldn't she have taken it more seriously instead of discarding it like a used napkin in the trash? No, this meant she'd received enough of them to consider this as more of a bark than bite. At least until something spooked her at Bullseye.

Raina grabbed a tissue and blotted off the congealing sauce. Grabbing another tissue, she carefully wrapped it around the note, making sure she didn't touch any more of the paper than necessary. She slipped it into the pocket of her jeans. If she left the note in the trash, it might not be there by the time the police got around to searching the place.

She clicked open the email program on the laptop. The messages were all in Chinese. She scanned the subject lines, looking for the personal emails. There seemed to be a fair number between Sui Yuk and Zhou Long Jun. While Raina spoke and understood enough Cantonese to order lunch at a Chinese restaurant, her knowledge of the written characters was on par with a beginning reader where the characters were a hit or miss depending on the context.

She glanced at the clock on the laptop. Lucille had been gone for fifteen minutes already. No time to puzzle out the Chinese characters. She snapped photo after photo of the messages. Her heart raced at the thought of Lucille returning before she could finish, lending her a rush of adrenaline that gave her tunnel vision. She opened the web browser's history and snapped a photo of the recent sites Sui Yuk visited and turned off the laptop.

Muffled laughter drifted in from the closed front door. Raina shut down the laptop and wiped off her fingerprints. She sprawled on the sofa and whipped out her cell phone.

The door opened, and Lucille strode in, flush and slightly breathless. "Please don't tell me you've been sitting here all this time."

Raina looked up, feigning surprise. "What? You said we were on break." She swung her legs around, leaning forward eagerly. "Guess what? My friend Stacy just got engaged. I can't believe this. Oh, Eden is going to be so jealous. Stacy is with her ex." She almost clapped her hands in front of her chest but decided it would be a little too much.

Lucille snorted in disgust. "You are here to work, not to gossip like a schoolgirl. Oh wait, you are a schoolgirl."

Raina flushed but ignored the barb. "I think we shouldn't touch anything in this room."

"Cecelia said—"

"No one has seen Sui Yuk Liang in the last twenty-four hours. All her stuff is still here.

Something could have happened to her. Let's just play it safe and not touch anything."

"Are you always such a drama queen?"

"Go see for yourself. Why would she leave her glasses or her laptop behind?"

Lucille walked into the bedroom. The back of her shirt was untucked.

Who came back from a smoking break looking like she had a tumble in a bounce house? This explained the goofy smile earlier. What nerve to call her a schoolgirl when Lucille was the one necking with a coworker while she should have been working. Maybe Lucille was poaching on Cecelia's boy toy. Raina shuddered. Yuck! There wasn't enough bleach in the world to clean the thought of Lucille gyrating with the pool boy from her brain.

Lucille came back into the room with a satisfied smile on her face. If she'd been a cat, her tail would be waving behind her. "We'll let Cecelia make the call. Let's get out of here."

They headed back to the utility room.

This time Raina pushed the maid's cart while Lucille walked next to her with a spring in her step. Her coworker had miraculously left her surly mood in Sui Yuk Liang's bedroom. What did she do in there?

Raina was loading one of the commercial washing machines with used towels when her cell phone dinged. The text message was from Matthew.

BREAKFAST TOMORROW? **I'**LL MAKE IT WORTH YOUR WHILE.

Raina rolled her eyes as she replied yes. Matthew always believed that if he talked a big game, she'd believe he was a skirt-chasing player. The persona he adopted around her was nothing more than a cover-up because of how much she frightened him. Of course, she let him continue with his delusion because it amused her. She knew he'd never push her outside her comfort zone. There was nothing wrong with a little flirting between two single friends.

Her phone dinged again. She opened the text app. The photo of the threatening note she'd sent earlier had failed to send. She hit the re-send button. She also tapped out a quick message to Po Po to let her know she would stop by with takeout for dinner.

A maintenance worker came into the room and grabbed several boxes off the wire racks on the far wall. He exchanged greetings in Spanish with Lucille. She rolled her eyes, but her wide smile was welcoming.

"I can finish up here," Lucille said.

Raina suppressed her smirk. "Thanks. *Hasta mañana.*"

Lucille gave her a steely look. "Get your mind out of the gutter."

"Trust me, I don't want to be anywhere near there."

As Raina strolled toward her car, she couldn't help but think her working relationship with Lucille was off to a roaring success.

It was only for two weeks. She could deal with it.

Raina squinted at the shadows of the parking lot behind the community room. Which row did she park in? In the dim light, all the cars were shades of gray and black. In another hour, the guests would congregate around the community room for dinner, but at this time the dead silence was unnerving. She shivered at the chill. Time to pick up some comfort food and go to her grandma's condo.

A dark car with bright headlights swung around the bend and the tires squealed at the too fast turn. Raina froze as it headed straight toward her. Her feet grew roots under the glare of the lights and the wind snapped her black curls against her face. For the first time, she finally understood what deer in head-lights meant.

The wind slammed something wet and slimy against her chest. Her hands automatically brushed it off, and the spell was broken.

She stumbled to the right, banging an elbow painfully against a parked van. She sucked in a breath, making herself as small as possible as she clutched her elbow in front of her. The dark car slid into the parking spot two feet away from her body, the engine idling.

Raina's throat tightened, allowing her to only make an eek sound like a mouse. She took several rattled breaths, but her heart continued to gallop. Carbon monoxide drifted into her nostrils and irritated the back of her throat. Another minute ticked by, and the driver still didn't come out to apologize. She clenched her jaw as her fright turned into irritation. *People like this shouldn't be driving.*

She stomped over to the driver's side and rapped on the window. Nothing. She pressed her lips into a thin line and knocked again. The window rolled down, and Cecelia's profile came into view. "You almost ran me over. Didn't you see me?"

Cecelia jerkily turned her head, as if she were a wooden puppet. Her eyes were wide, the pupils dilated. Her hands still clamped on the steering wheel. She opened her mouth, but no sound came out.

Raina took a step back, gooseflesh peppering her arms. The resort owner was a sickly shade of gray in the dim light. "Are you okay?"

Cecelia blinked several times, staring through Raina. "I can't believe she's dead. How can she be dead?"

The world stood still as a sense of deja vu swept over Raina. Through numb lips, she whispered, "Who's dead?"

Cecelia shook as if awakening from a dream. "One of our guests. Sui Yuk Liang. The police asked me to identify her personal effects."

Raina stumbled as if the resort owner had just slapped her. She'd been right, but there was no sense of validation or triumph. The young mother had left her baby with a stranger out of sheer desperation. "How did she die?"

Cecelia got out of the car. Her wild eyes focused on Raina. "She got hit by a car. I can't believe she's gone. I didn't even need to make plans after all." She lurched toward her office.

Raina watched the resort owner walk away. What plans was Cecelia talking about? Did someone intentionally run Sui Yuk down? She hurried to her car as the shadows closed in around her. She was very much aware that the threatening note in her pocket could be the only link to a murderer.

TAKE MY KIDNEY

Water and mud squished under Raina's shoes as she made her way into the senior condo complex attached to the Gold Springs Senior Center. She hugged the plastic bag of take-out food against her body as she leapt over a puddle and ran to the entrance of the building from her car. She didn't bother waiting for the elevator and ran up the three flights of stairs. Knocking with rapid taps, she shook the plastic bag until water sluiced onto the carpeted floor in the hall.

Po Po opened the door. "Rainy, what a surprise." Her eyes lit up when she saw the takeout bag. "And you got food."

Raina stepped into the neat two-bedroom condo. "Didn't you get my text message? I sent it before I left the resort." She didn't tell her grandma that she sent the message after Matthew rejected her dinner plans. It wasn't like Po Po was filler, but she was second choice for the evening.

Po Po closed the door. "I didn't get a text."

Raina set the food on the dining room table. She pulled out her phone and opened her text app. Sure enough, the message to her grandma bounced back with a network error, but at least the photo of the threatening note went through to Matthew. She hit the re-send key and somewhere in the condo a cell phone dinged. "My phone hasn't worked properly since the drop at Bullseye. I need to stop by the cell phone store tomorrow after work."

Po Po went into the kitchen and came back with two place settings. Her grandma might not cook, but she didn't eat out of takeout cartons like a savage. According to her grandma, there was always time for a proper sit-down dinner even if someone else made it.

Raina shoved food into her mouth as if she'd just gotten off a hunger strike. Fear always made her eat like she was storing it up for later.

Po Po put down her fork. "Okay, what is going on? You always get that squirrel look when something is really bothering you. Tell me what it is before you end up eating my meal too."

Raina gulped water and sighed, content with the slight bulge in her stomach. She discreetly unbuttoned her jeans under her shirt.

"That bad, huh? Is Matthew jerking you around again? I'm going to have a talk with Maggie about this. I'm—"

Raina was hoping her grandma wouldn't notice the button. "It's not Matthew. Please"—she held up her hands—"stay out of this. Matthew and I are adults. We don't need our grandmas to help us figure anything out. Don't embarrass me, okay?"

Po Po harrumphed. "Fine. I don't see what's so embarrassing about me talking to my best friend—"

"Thank you."

"If it's about the family dinner—"

"It's about the poor abandoned baby. Well, it's about his mother... or at least I think she was his mom." Raina told her grandma everything that happened at the resort, starting with the supposed stillbirth, the threatening note, and the news of Sui Yuk's death.

Her grandma's eyes grew wider and wider. "This almost sounds like a soap opera. It almost feels like the cosmos is pushing you toward this baby."

It was her feeling exactly. "What if Aaron Wheeler has something to do with Sui Yuk's death? What if he is BL's father, and this was a simple custody battle gone wrong?"

"But this wouldn't explain the stillbirth.

And don't forget, BL doesn't look like a mixed baby. Where is the threatening note?"

"It's in my glove compartment. I didn't want to haul it around in the rain. The less it gets handled, the better. I would have left it in the trash can except I'm not sure it would still be there by the time the cops decide to investigate this."

"Do you think BL's parents sent the threatening note?"

"I don't know what to believe. Lucille could be lying to me, but so could everyone who has any interest in the baby. Maybe the answers are in Sui Yuk's emails. Where's your laptop? You can probably translate the Chinese characters quicker and more accurately than I could."

Po Po pointed to her bedroom. "The USB cord for my phone is in there too. On the dresser."

Raina retrieved the laptop and cell phone cord while her grandma finished up her meal. It was a good thing both their cell phones had the same connector. Within minutes she downloaded all the photos onto her grandma's laptop. "You know what I find strange? It's Cecelia's offhanded comment about making plans."

"Maybe it has to do with Sui Yuk blabbing about her stillbirth. This could impact business. Who wants to give birth at a place cursed with miscarriages and stillbirths?"

"Cursed?"

Po Po gave her a sheepish smile. "So I'm a little melodramatic here. It's been several months since I've had to dodge flying bullets."

"What bullets?"

"Well, Olivia Kline waved a loaded gun around. So, technically the bullets were flying."

Her grandma was referring to their investigation on her college adviser's death a few months ago. A drunk waving a gun around threatening to shoot raccoons wasn't "dodging flying bullets."

"I wonder if there's any record of the stillbirth at the birth clinic," Raina said.

"Can't you just pop over and have a look-see tomorrow?"

Raina shook her head. "The clinic is on the north end of the property. It is advertised as a boutique birth clinic on the Internet. They have their own janitorial service that comes in after hours."

Po Po rubbed her hands together. "This sounds like I might have to do some undercover work."

"Oh no, you don't. Just let me see what I can find out first. Last time you helped me you ended up with a sprained ankle."

Her grandma flexed her foot. "No real harm done. Do you know how many dinner parties I was invited to just so the other seniors could live vicariously through me? Trust me, I'm not doing you any favors."

"You don't think we should leave this to the police?" Raina asked. "Matthew is good at his job."

"Even if Matthew wants to investigate this, there will be political pressure for him to just wrap it up. It'd take a strong man to stand up and do the right thing in this case."

Raina had feared as much when she found out Sui Yuk Liang was a foreign tourist. She doubted if anyone in either country wanted to look too closely at this. It was far less work for everyone if Sui Yuk's death was a simple hit-and-run accident and BL was her son. Far easier. But it didn't make it right. And there was BL's safety to worry about. What if whoever killed Sui Yuk was now after the baby?

"Are you going to call Eden?" Po Po asked.

"She's out of town. It's not my job to go sniff out stories for her." Besides, her friend might spin this into an international PR nightmare if given half the chance.

THEY WERE in the middle of an episode of *Big Bang Theory* when Cassie called. Raina excused herself and stepped into her grandma's spare bedroom.

"Rainy, is this a good time to talk?" Cassie asked.

When did her sister ask to talk? Cassie always started yakking before Raina even said hello. "Sure. I was just watching TV with Po Po."

"Okay."

There was a long pause, and Raina was on the brink of saying hello again when she heard her sister take a deep breath.

"Can you loan me twenty thousand dollars?" Cassie asked.

Raina blinked in surprise. This was the first time her sister had ever asked her for a loan. "I don't have that much cash in my checking account. What do you need the money for?"

"I can wait a couple of days. You probably need to move money around."

It'd require more than a couple of days to cash out her meager retirement account. "If it's urgent, you may have better luck with our grandma."

"I'm too embarrassed to ask Po Po. I want to pay off our credit cards. The twenty-one percent interest rate is killing us."

"Is something wrong?" Raina gasped as a thought struck her. "Are you sick? Is it Lila?"

Cassie laughed nervously. "Everyone is fine. Nothing is wrong. We just have bills to pay."

Her sister wasn't normally so irresponsible with money. "Oh."

"Don't you dare judge me," Cassie said with a sharp tone. "What is your problem? I'm sure you get more than twenty thousand dollars in interest from the money Ah Gong left you. Not all of us woke up one day with a boatload of cash like you did."

Raina's stomach twisted into pretzel knots. When did her sister start drinking from the same Kool-Aid cup as her cousins? More than anything else, Raina wished she could confide in her sister about their granddad's secret. "I'd give you the money from the inheritance if I could, but it's slated for something else. It's not my secret to tell even if I'm one of its keepers. But once I'm free to tell you, I know you'd understand."

Cassie groaned. "Oh, Raina, you're such a drama queen. It's not like I'm asking for one of your kidneys."

Lila cried in the background, and her sister set the phone down. She soothed her daughter with a patient voice that was more like her normal self.

Cassie picked up the phone again. "I don't have time to talk anymore." And she hung up without saying good-bye.

Raina bit her lower lip to stop it from trembling. Like the rest of her cousins, Cassie had only gotten one dollar from their grandfather. Her support had been the keystone that kept Raina going this past year when the rest of the family had turned against her.

Why did everyone eventually abandon her? First, Matthew and his "I love you, but I can't be with you" and now Cassie and her "My love comes at a price." Raina sighed. The topper would be a phone call from her mom asking for a new car. Why couldn't someone just ask for something simple, like a kidney?

SMALL TOWN U.S.A.

After a sleepless night of wrestling with her covers and dreaming of a crying Lila held over a boiling cauldron by a laughing Aaron Wheeler, Raina was more than ready to get an early start on her day. She had two hours to kill before she had to leave to meet Matthew for breakfast.

As she waited for her hazelnut coffee to brew, she pulled out several bricks of cream cheese so it could soften on the countertop. One never knew when a cheesecake could come in handy. As pathetic as it was to admit, her cooking had gotten her further than her looks ever did. By the time she left her apartment, the raspberry chocolate cheesecake was nestled next to her shrimp wontons in the freezer. And things were looking better already with a belly full of chocolate chips.

The short drive to the Venus Café was pleasant, full of twinkling lights softened by a light drizzle and relaxing Christmas music from the radio. Raina had initially moved to Gold Springs to escape her large family in San Francisco, but the small college town worked its magic on her and she could no longer imagine living anywhere else. Even her grandma, a lifelong city dweller, couldn't resist the temptation of friendly neighbors, small mom-and-pop shops, and a healthy local economy.

A few minutes later, she parked in front of the olive green bungalow with white trim on the corner of Main Street and Second Avenue. The café featured half a dozen small tables and a large fireplace surrounded by cracked leather reading chairs.

For a Monday morning, the place was dead. Was everyone out of town or sleeping in? Brenda, her friend and the owner, had eye bags the size of saucers, but her smile was warm and friendly as ever. She waved to Raina from behind the counter but rolled her eyes at the far corner where Matthew sat next to a window framed with a multi-colored strand of lights. He didn't appear to even notice the floor-to-ceiling murals of handsome men frolicking next to naked nymphs with strategically placed flowing hair or bits of leaves.

Matthew had on his police department-issued navy-colored polo shirt. The bomber jacket she'd given him some years ago hung on the back of the chair. It had been three months since they had last spent time alone together, and she wasn't sure if her heart was still safe when she was around him. They said old habits die hard, and Matthew was a habit from her high school years she should have outgrown by now.

He gave her a beaming smile, and she had to swallow the knot that formed in her throat. "I ordered for us already. Peppermint latte and wild rice chicken soup with a small crusty baguette. Your winter favorite."

Raina glanced at the food on the table and gave him a tight smile. So what if he remembered her seasonal favorite food. As far as she was concerned, it was a little too little, and a little too late. They had spent the last ten years tumbling into bed each time their lives intersected, from Rome to Las Vegas. And each time someone cried, blood got spilled, and things blew up. Even their recent encounter in town involved a dead body. If she were an adrenaline junkie, Matthew would be her perfect fix.

"Did you get the photo I sent you last night?" Raina asked.

"What photo?" Matthew asked.

Raina pulled out the threatening note

from her purse. It was in a little Ziploc bag just like in the crime shows. "It's a photo of this. I found it in the trashcan of Sui Yuk Liang's room. I didn't want it to get thrown out accidentally, so I took it." She watched him read the note and the smile disappeared from his face. "I also know Sui Yuk Liang is dead. In light of this recent development, don't you think there is now enough evidence to suspect foul play?"

He put the note in the pocket of his jacket. "Now how did you find out about the hit-and-run? Is it Donna—"

"Cecelia," Raina cut in. She didn't want Donna to get in trouble since the front desk clerk at the police station was always more than happy to trade gossip for food. "Are there tire marks to identify—"

"Rainy, do you think this is appropriate breakfast conversation? You talk about her death as if you were buying a new pair of shoes."

Raina sipped her latte to hide her confusion. Had she become jaded with death? She felt a lingering sadness for Sui Yuk Liang, but she was more anxious for BL's safety.

"I'm really concerned about the baby, Matthew." Raina told him about Sui Yuk's supposed stillbirth. "So who does BL actually belong to?"

"Who is BL?"

"The baby—"

"You named him? You're not supposed—"

"He is not a stray dog. Just because I named him doesn't mean I get to keep him."

He raised an eyebrow. "With the gray skies and wet weather yesterday, the driver probably didn't see her. The only lead we got is a partial print of a tire in the mud. The driver might have pulled over, but then got scared and took off."

Her stomach tightened at the image in her head. What if the person pulled over to make sure Sui Yuk was actually dead? She took a deep breath. Her imagination was galloping faster than a bullet train. "So there is no possibility of foul play?"

"There's always the possibility, but I have a feeling there's going to be pressure to ship the kid to China ASAP. This means, they want an open and shut case. A foreign tourist got killed in a traffic accident. Simple. Easy. The FBI contacts the Chinese embassy, who would then contact the Liang family."

"But it's not that simple. Have you forgotten about Aaron Wheeler? What about the threatening note?"

Matthew sighed as he ran his hands through his hair, causing the ends to spike up. "This could turn into a political nightmare for our town. Trust me, you really don't want to get involved in this. I am so thankful your friend Eden is out of town. Can you imagine what she could do with this story?"

Raina ignored his dig on her best friend. Eden was the Assistant Chief-in-Editor for *Gold Springs Weekly*, their small newspaper that ran once a week with the occasional special edition run. Matthew didn't trust Eden and for good reason. Sometimes Eden could be offensive and less than tactful when dealing with the police, but then wasn't that part of being a reporter?

"You're going to stand by and let BL go to the wrong family?" she asked.

"This is not my call to make. And I don't see what is the big deal. He'll still go to a family that is expecting a baby," he said.

Raina gritted her teeth to give herself a moment to calm down. Of course, he wouldn't think it was a big deal. Here was a man who didn't value the bonds of a family. Both his parents had abandoned him before he was even done with first grade.

"Being with the wrong family is a big deal. BL would grow up wondering why he doesn't look like his parents or why he doesn't quite fit in his family. He needs to be with his real mother, who is probably searching for him right now. And what if he's not even a Chinese citizen?"

"Rainy, you're over thinking this."

"No, you're under thinking this."

"Once the FBI takes over the case, I'm not going to be able to protect you. And the feds don't take kindly to nosy civilians meddling in their investigation."

Raina flushed at his tone. Meddling? She didn't meddle. "If it weren't for me—"

"Trouble will keep knocking on your door if you keep rolling out the welcome mat." His gold-flecked brown eyes studied her with concern.

Raina gave him a self-deprecating smile. "What can I say? I'm an adrenaline junkie."

"I'm sure you'll be nosing around the resort no matter what I say." Matthew rubbed his temples. "I should just slap a GPS tracker on your butt and get it over with."

"My butt is no longer your concern."

"Your butt is of the utmost concern to me."

"Will you stop it?"

His eyes twinkled. "Stop what?"

"Why are you playing cat and mouse with

me? When I finally accept that you don't want a relationship with me, you're flirting like you want to start something again. If you care for me at all, you'd stop."

The smile disappeared from his face. "I'm sorry. This is completely new to me as well. I just haven't quite figured out how to act when I'm around you."

"What are you trying to say?" She winced internally at the catch in her voice.

He replied slowly, pronouncing each word so there was no mistaking its meaning. "I'm an idiot. The last thing I want to do is to hurt you. And I just realized that if I keep this up, I would. I've already told you I don't think I have what it takes to be the family man you deserve—"

"But how would you know until we really tried?"

He shook his head. "There's more—"

"Arh, hello?" said a soft feminine voice next to them.

No, no, no! Getting a man to talk about his

feelings was even harder than finding the right pair of jeans to flatter her butt. Didn't this woman notice the "do not disturb" vibe around them? Raina glanced up, barely suppressing the scowl on her face. Fanny. Really? At a time like this?

Fanny's wide eyes smiled at her from a heart-shaped face framed by black hair with pink highlights. "I hope I'm not interrupting."

Raina glanced at Matthew. Of course he'd notice the cute foreign exchange student. She tucked a loose curl back into her boring pony-tail. Not that she was jealous.

"Fanny, this is... ah, my friend, Matthew," Raina said. The bell attached to the front door jingled, and a draft of cold air swirled around her legs. She shivered, and just as quickly the draft was gone.

The foreign exchange student dropped her gaze as her cheeks flushed. When she peeked at him from under lowered lashes, her glance had enough flames to light up a Christmas tree.

Raina pressed her lips together. What was she? Fermented seaweed? You didn't poach on another woman's boyfriend until said woman was out of the picture. Ex. She'd meant to say ex-boyfriend.

"I'm sorry about yesterday. I missed the bus." Fanny pulled out a chair and sat as if she was preparing for an extended visit. "I was going to ask Joe for a ride, but he... ah, had an emergency."

Raina forced herself to be gracious. "Don't worry about it."

As if Fanny's presence was an indication they were rolling out the welcome mat, Brenda appeared with another iced coffee and set it in front of Raina. "Want to come over for dinner tomorrow night? There's someone I want you to meet." She lowered her voice into a stage whisper. "He's a cutie."

Raina bit her lip to stop the laughter from spilling out. What a twist. Here was Fanny batting her lashes at Matthew, while Brenda was trying to set her up. And why not? Even before the interruption, Matthew was telling her yet again that he wasn't emotionally available to her. She had to move on. It was naiveté to believe she could change a man by being a wet bath mat. "Sure."

"Great," said Brenda. "Seven o'clock." At Raina's nod, she strolled into the kitchen.

Fanny smiled at Raina, as if she were in on a secret. "Oh, you're in for a treat. Especially if you like them squishy and drooling." She laughed like a chorus of broken champagne flutes.

Matthew looked relieved. "I take it he's not good looking? Maybe a little dull."

Fanny shrugged her slim shoulders. "He doesn't say much, and what comes out is not worth talking about."

Raina shifted in her chair. What if this guy Brenda wanted her to meet was another dud? No, her friend wouldn't do that to her. Would she? Great, now Matthew and Fanny were buddy-buddy over her supposed blind date.

Matthew's face was openly curious. "Your

English is rather good. I'm surprised you're here to learn English."

"Actually, I'm a U.S. citizen. I went to Stanford for my undergrad work." Fanny paused as if waiting for them to fall off their chairs in surprise. When nothing happened, she continued, "I like America. And since I'm not married, I told my parents I'm here to catch a rich American husband."

Raina snickered. "There's no rich husband at this table."

"Maybe American is enough."

Raina could feel her blood pressure rising. Maybe American was enough. Maybe you need to turn off those bedroom eyes. She gave Matthew a sideways glance, only to find him already studying her with amusement. He knew exactly what Fanny's comments were doing to her. The jerk.

"You have dual citizenship? Which parent is from the States?" Matthew asked. His tone was neutral and friendly.

"Neither. My mom was on vacation in Los Angeles when she gave birth to me."

Raina straightened. This sounded like the guests at the Gold Springs Birth Resort. "You have a U.S. citizenship, but you don't live here?"

"Yes. I have access to some of the best colleges without having to pay the international fees. I have a U.S. passport, so I can travel everywhere. When I'm here, I work part-time, so I can claim Social Security later. Wealthier families try to have their baby in the U.S."

"Is this even legal?"

"Birth tourism is a shadow industry in the U.S., but it's heavily advertised in Asia." Fanny leaned forward and lowered her voice. "I don't think your government wants to do anything about this loophole because of the tourist dollars."

"And you say all your friends are like you?"

Fanny looked at her hands as if trying to

appear modest. "Only those that can afford it."

"Do you want to live here full time?" Matthew asked.

"Not really. Well, maybe with the right man," Fanny said, giving him another smoldering look. "My family and friends are in China. I just need to escape once in a while."

"Why here? It's not like there's a lot to do in Gold Springs," Raina said.

"Small town U.S.A. I thought it might be charming, but if Bullseye was the best shopping experience Gold Springs has to offer..." Fanny trailed off.

Raina blushed. So Fanny did know better. She should have known a village girl wouldn't have the means to travel to another country because she found her normal life dull. "It's a small town." She cringed at the sharp tone in her voice.

Matthew threw his crumpled napkin on his plate. "I'll leave you to your girl-talk." His eyes twinkled at Raina. "Let me know if you find anything at the resort."

Fanny watched him leave. "They don't make men like that in China." She glanced at Raina. "Is he single?"

8

LIBEL AND SLANDER

Later that afternoon, Raina kept a lookout for Cecelia while she cleaned the suites with Lucille. When she saw the resort owner heading toward her office, she suggested a break. Lucille readily agreed, trailing a whiff of cigarette smoke in her wake as she jogged toward the Community Room.

Raina trotted after Cecelia without any idea on how to broach the subject of Sui Yuk's baby. She knocked on the opened door. "Hi, Cecelia. How are you holding up?"

Cecelia glanced up from her laptop screen. While her manly features and countenance still conveyed an impression of vigorous health, her eye bags and the set of her mouth told a different story. "I'm fine. Why?"

"Don't you remember what happened last night? You were so agitated, you almost ran me over."

"Sorry about that. I had a lot of things on my mind." Cecelia gave a suggestion of a smile, a tight curl at the corners that was more effort than impact. "No harm, no foul, right?"

Raina grimaced, rolling up her sleeve to display the impressive bruise on her elbow. Cecelia didn't have to know she'd darkened it with make-up. "I promise I won't sue." The resort owner would have to play nice at least for a little while.

Cecelia's smile turned sickly. "It wasn't intentional."

"Of course not. After all, you just came back from identifying Sui Yuk Liang's things. I would be distracted too if I were in your shoes."

Cecelia's eyes darted to the open doorway behind Raina. She lowered her voice. "I don't want to talk about Ms. Liang. She was a demanding guest, and we were more than happy to see her leave."

"But she didn't leave. Lucille and I were supposed to pack up her things yesterday. Why is her stuff still at the resort? Who has custody of her baby?"

Cecelia froze as her fingers curled like talons above the keyboard. "What are you talking about?"

Raina's eyes widened as a sudden thought hit her. Cecelia must have helped Sui Yuk Liang steal the baby from another woman. It was the only explanation. Sui Yuk wouldn't have been able to pass BL off as hers without help. But how did she get Cecelia to commit such a crime? Blackmail?

"There was a crib in her room," Raina said. "I'm assuming she gave birth at the

Women Wellness and Birth Clinic. She doesn't have any family here, so who is taking care of the baby?"

"Are you an ambulance chaser? Are you that reporter, Eden Small?"

"No. I'm not Eden."

"Then why are you interested in Sui Yuk's death?"

"I don't even know her, if that's what you're asking. But I'm concerned there's a helpless baby out there. Do we need to notify the authorities that an orphaned baby might need our help?"

"And just what do you suggest? The police didn't mention her baby. I'm assuming someone took custody of him."

"But shouldn't we let the police or CPS know that the baby's family is in China? They would just naturally assume his parents are from around here."

"I would think growing up in the U.S. is preferable to China. There are a lot of advantages to having a U.S. citizenship."

Was this guilt talking? Or did she seriously think having material things was a substitute for the love of his parents? And did she as good as admit BL belonged to another woman? "But what about his family? Eventually his family would come knocking. Someone out there has to be looking for this child."

"Not my problem."

"You're a mother. Doesn't this bother you?"

"Nope. Not my child."

"It would be if the rumors spread about the stillbirths. I heard the baby didn't even belong to Sui Yuk." Raina tapped her chin. "I wonder where she got this baby if it's not hers."

"Let me assure you, there was no stillbirth. She had a little blood in her underwear, so her doctor recommended bed rest at a nearby hospital. Like I said, Sui Yuk wasn't well liked. I'm not surprised at the rumors, but there's just no truth to it."

"So she spent a month at Gold Springs General?" Raina asked.

"I can't divulge confidential information about our guests." Cecelia glanced at the clock on the wall. "You need to get back to work."

"I didn't realize the Gold Country Birth Resort had such a stellar reputation overseas. No wonder you don't want any rumors to circulate regarding the recent bout of stillbirths here. Sui Yuk wasn't the only one who ended up with a stillbirth after a stay here."

Cecelia paled as she shook with anger. "You're here to clean. Not make libelous comments about my business. Now keep your mouth shut and just go do your job."

"Actually it would be slander."

"What?"

Raina hung her head, hoping she looked contrite as she rubbed her elbow. Her questions hit a nerve. The resort owner definitely had something to hide, but it could be as innocent as protecting her business from rumors of stillbirth.

Cecelia took a rattled breath. "Sorry about losing my temper. The holidays are just so difficult for me." Her voice cracked. "I just don't need this added stress."

There was a knock at the doorway. Raina turned to find Matthew and Officer Hopper watching them. How long had they been standing there?

Matthew came into the office. "Cecelia Wagner? I'm Detective Matthew Louie and this is Officer Joanna Hopper."

The resort owner glanced at Raina. "You should probably get back to work."

Matthew ignored Raina, but Officer Hopper raised an eyebrow at her passing. Raina left the office, but outside the open doorway, she bent over her shoes, untying both laces.

Cecelia asked, "What can I do for you, Detective?"

"We would like to take a look at Sui Yuk Liang's room," Matthew said.

"Do you have a search warrant?" Cecelia asked.

Raina grabbed a shoelace. One bunny ear. Two bunny ears. A loopy loop. Pull, and one shoelace tied.

"No, but I can get one pretty quickly. It's much easier if you cooperate. It's not like you have anything to do with Sui Yuk Liang's death or have anything to hide, right?" Matthew said.

Cecelia gave a nervous laugh. "Of course not, but you can't just come and search my resort."

Raina grabbed the other shoelace and made bunny ears again as she tied them together.

"We're not asking to search your resort," Officer Hopper said, her voice soft and sweet. "We just want to take a look at Sui Yuk's room before you pack things up."

"Oh, all right. But you only get ten minutes. I have to make a call soon."

"I'll need Sui Yuk's registration information and any emergency contact information she gave you," Matthew said. "I'm assuming you have a standard package of forms for your guests to fill out. Was her baby born at Gold Springs General? I'd need a copy of the birth certificate and his mother's travel papers."

Cecelia's voice became strained. "Do I need a lawyer after all? You seem to be asking for more than my cooperation."

"This is just standard procedure," he said. "I'm collecting what information I can before the FBI gets here. This case could make international news and we're trying to get the baby home ASAP. I'm sure you wouldn't want this kind of news to be associated with your business."

"You have ten minutes in her room, but I'm calling my lawyer after this." A chair scraped against the floor. "I need to protect myself and my business."

Raina jogged around the corner as they

left the office. Matthew turned around just as they were about to disappear from view and wagged his index finger as if he knew Raina had been listening in the entire time. Oh boy. She was in for it now.

RAINA PULLED out her cell phone and texted Lucille to ask if she was done with her break. A couple seconds later, Lucille replied she needed ten more minutes. This was exactly the response Raina was hoping for.

POLICE HERE. IF I'M NOT IN ONE OF THE SUITES, I'M ANSWERING QUESTIONS.

Raina casually swerved her head to make sure Cecelia and the police didn't circle back. She slipped back into the office and closed the door. Her phone dinged again—a text message from Lucille.

WAITING UNTIL U GET BACK. NOT WORKING W/O U.

Why was she not surprised?

She stuffed the phone back into her pocket, while her other hand reached for the tall filing cabinet next to Cecelia's desk. Locked. She tried the other drawers on the desk, but they too were locked. Just great.

Raina glanced at the closed door, straining her ears to detect any sound. No footsteps. Another five minutes. She opened the closet, expecting boxes and a jacket or purse, and stifled a gasp of surprise.

A tall, slender Chinese woman in her thirties hid behind a purple parka. Her eyes showed more white than brown as breaths came out in noisy puffs. Her hands clutched the thin gold chain around her neck.

Raina took a deep breath to steady herself. The woman looked more like a mouse than a predator. "Who are you? And what are you doing in Cecelia's closet?"

Footsteps approached the office. Someone was coming. The mouse woman squeezed her eyes shut, mumbling a prayer in Chinese.

Raina's eyes flicked to the window. No time to wrestle it open. Couldn't hide under the desk. She jumped inside the closet and closed the door. Trapped. She wanted to join the mouse woman in her prayers.

The door opened and a chair squeaked. Rose perfume seeped in from the gaps around the door. It didn't take a brain surgeon to guess that Cecelia had returned to her office.

Raina's eyes itched. She hated it when perfume used real ingredients instead of the fake stuff. Her fingers shook when she pulled out her cell phone from her pocket. It squirted out of her hand like a slick bar of soap. She reached for it, but it danced on her fingers and bounced off. Time slowed, and her heart stopped beating.

The phone flipped through the air and landed on the mouse woman's chest. She slapped both hands to her chest and held onto the phone. She blinked as if surprised at her own dexterity. Without a word, she held it out.

Raina's heart resumed its normal tempo. Mouthing "thank you," she reached for the phone. She turned off the ringer and texted Po Po.

Help! Trapped inside Cecelia's office closet. Call to say you have message for Hopper.

The mouse woman continued to mouth prayers.

"Be quiet," Raina whispered in Chinese.

The mouse woman sank silently to the floor. It didn't look like Raina would get any help from her.

The phone in the office rang, and Raina held her breath.

"Hello, Gold Country Birth Resort," Cecelia said. The chair squeaked again. "Yes, Officer Hopper is still here."

Silence.

"How do I know whether or not her phone is working?"

Silence.

"Don't you have a radio you can use?"

Cecelia sighed. "Oh, alright. Hold on." The chair squeaked and footsteps grew fainter as she left the room.

Raina pumped her fist in the air. She took a deep breath and cracked the door. No sound in the office. Swinging the door open, she grabbed her companion's arm and hustled them outside. When they left the building, the Chinese woman tried to shake off Raina's hand.

Oh no, you don't. Raina tightened her grip. "Who are you, and what are you doing in Cecelia's office?" she asked in Chinese.

"I could ask you the same thing," the mouse woman said, scowling now that the immediate threat of discovery was over.

Raina studied the woman. Chin length bob, narrow face, tiny brown eyes, and the soft squishy look in the stomach area of someone who had recently given birth. Her eyes widened. Could this be BL's birth mother?

Her cell phone screen lit up. She glanced down to find a text message from her grandma. The split second was enough for the mouse woman to run across the lawn toward the Community Room.

Raina hightailed it after the woman. "Wait!" Rounding the corner of the building, she slammed into the maid's cart.

White towels spilled onto the muddy ground, tiny shampoo bottles clattered against the side of the building, and toilet paper rolls flew up into the air. Raina landed on her hip, and a sharp pain radiated up her backside.

"Oh my God!" Lucille said, reaching for Raina's hands. "Are you okay?"

Raina closed her eyes and sat in the mud for another second. "Where is the ice machine located again?"

9

KISSY KISS, YUCKY POO

After finishing her shift, Raina had just enough time to stop by the cell phone store to see what she could do about her cracked phone. She limped into the store, nursing her bruised hip. Icing had helped, but what she needed was a long soak in a tub. And a chat with Po Po about the woman hiding in Cecelia's office.

The place was packed. Sardines had more breathing room. A sales associate in his thirties with a bristly mustache with more hair on his face than his head approached her and asked for her name and cell phone number.

Her luck was finally turning around. She didn't know what she did to skip to the head of the line, but she wasn't questioning it. Maybe her ancestors were rewarding her for trying to help an innocent baby. After rattling off her information, she said, "I dropped my phone a few days ago, and it hasn't been reliable since. My messages—"

"Sorry, madam," said Mr. Mustache. "I'm just the greeter. You're number thirteen on the waiting list. We'll call you when it's your turn."

Madam? The guy was older than her. Raina swallowed her flash of disappointment. So she didn't win the lottery after all. "How long is the wait?"

He shrugged in a careless way that suggested he didn't really care. "Depends on what the people ahead of you want. It's the final shopping week before Christmas. Everyone is looking for that last minute gift."

Raina ground her teeth. She wanted to close her eyes and scream. Why were all these people waiting until the last minute to shop? It wasn't like they didn't know Christmas happened every year.

"Hey, you okay? You look like you're about to have a hernia," Mr. Mustache said.

Serenity now. Serenity now. "I'm just having a bad day." She held up her phone.

He whistled at the cracked screen.

"Exactly. The phone works only when the stars are aligned and I've sacrificed a pygmy goat. I need something more reliable," Raina said.

Mr. Mustache tapped on the screen. "There's two more months left on your contract, and you don't have insurance on your phone. You either can pay for the full cost of a new smart phone or you can pay the termination fee to end your contract early."

"Both options cost more than my two months of service. How about a dumb phone?"

"You can look around while you wait. Even the cheapest phone is over a hundred dollars." He lowered his voice and stepped closer. "But I can hook you up."

Raina raised an eyebrow as she studied him. Free lunches were like the abominable snowman. No one could supply any proof either existed. "What's it going to cost me?"

"Nothing. As a matter of fact, you get a free dinner"—he stroked his mustache and the tip of his tongue darted out to lick his chapped lips—"and maybe dessert if you're a good girl."

Raina stiffened in distaste. For a half second she was *this close* to saying yes. "I wouldn't know how to be good even if my life depended on it."

He smirked. "Oh, I like a bad girl."

She turned around and left the store.

"I'll call you," Mr. Mustache called after her.

Raina shuddered as the glass door closed

behind her. Was this customer service at its best during the holidays? Her phone would just have to limp along until after Christmas. It wasn't like she really needed a phone. Back in the day, people had to rely on pay phones and pagers, and the world didn't stop spinning then.

WHILE THE COFFEE BREWED, Raina unpacked the groceries. She had forty minutes to whip something up for dinner. A cold winter night like this called for comfort food—shrimp wonton soup with bok choy. Yum.

Standing dinner dates with her grandma turned out surprisingly symbiotic. Po Po got home-cooked meals and often left with a doggie bag while Raina got free groceries. It was a match made in gastric heaven.

Her mom approved of Raina's interest in cooking. She believed the best way to get a man to stay was to plump him up so he had no options. Call her picky, but Raina's ideal soul mate wasn't Humpty Dumpty.

She was chopping the bok choy when someone knocked on the front door. It couldn't be Po Po because her grandma had a key. She grabbed the pepper spray from her purse on the way to the door. If Aaron Wheeler tracked her down, then he was stupider than she thought. She wasn't Po Po's favorite granddaughter for nothing.

Raina looked through the peephole, but the condensation from the rain fogged the lens. She squinted. Was the person a man or a woman?

The person knocked again.

She curled a finger on the trigger of the pepper spray and opened the door.

The tall rotund woman with a thick silver braid held up her hands when she caught sight of the pepper spray. "My name is Toni Moody. I'm a private investigator. If this isn't a good time, I'll come back later." She slowly withdrew a business card from her purse as if facing a wild hog ready to charge.

Raina accepted the card and tucked it into her pocket without glancing at it. With technology these days, anyone could print a bogus business card from home. "What can I do for you, Toni? As you can see, I'm rather jumpy right now, so let's make this quick."

"I'm investigating the Gold Country Birth Resort for a client. I'm hoping you can answer some questions for me."

Raina narrowed her eyes in suspicion. "Do you have spies at the resort? It's rather early for my place of employment to show up on any Internet search."

"No spies. I spoke with your friend, Sonia Cardenas, I mean Sonia Cruz now, before she left for her honeymoon. She said you might be amenable to answering some questions about the resort."

Raina lowered her pepper spray. So maybe

this Toni Moody wasn't a foe...yet. "Are you working with Aaron Wheeler?"

Toni's deep blue eyes appeared violet in the dim light. They were without guile. "I have never heard of this person. Sorry, but due to confidentiality, I can't tell you who my client is."

Raina inhaled sharply as a tingling sensation started in the back of her head. "Are you investigating Cecelia?"

Toni inclined her head, which could be interpreted as a yes or an acknowledgment of the question. "Ms. Sun, have you met any of the doctors or nurses at the Women Wellness and Birth Clinic?"

Raina shook her head.

"Do you know if any of the employees are undocumented workers?"

Lucille's face flashed in front of her. Her coworker was too lazy to be undocumented. Nope, her coworker was too secure in her job. "None that I'm aware of. Who else have you talked to?"

"Just Sonia and you as of now. Do you interact with the guests?"

"Na-ah. Why this interest in the employment practices at the resort? Are you with the feds?"

Toni ignored her questions. "Do you notice any kind of unusual activity at the resort?"

"It's not that I'm trying to be unhelpful, but I just started." And why should Raina answer all the questions when Toni wasn't in the mood to share?

"You have my card. Give me a call if anything turns up."

After the private investigator left and while the chicken broth simmered, Raina searched for the private investigator on her laptop. There were several hits plus a headshot of the woman. She ignored the business websites for now and scanned the few news articles. Then she went on California's Department of Consumer Affairs website and typed in "Moody Investigations." It came back with a clear and current valid license.

She sat back on her sofa and stared at the ticking koi clock above her TV. Toni appeared to be exactly who she said she was. But who was her client? And why this interest in the employment practices at the resort?

Raina was setting the table when her grandma sailed through the front door.

Po Po eyed the steaming bowls and rubbed her hands together as if she were auditioning to be one of Pavlov's dogs. "Need any help?"

Raina wanted to snort. Her grandma called the gap between the kitchen and the stove "The Grand Canyon." To put it politely, cooking wasn't her forte. "Why don't you get us something to drink?"

Po Po gave her a smart salute. "Aye-aye, Batman."

Raina told her grandma about Toni Moody's visit. "What do you think is going on?"

"Definitely something shady. This makes

Sui Yuk Liang's death seem more and more like a homicide."

"How is the translation of the emails going?" Raina asked.

Po Po opened her mouth and stuck a finger inside, pretending to barf. "Painful. I'm halfway through, but it's nothing more than sappy love letters to her husband. I'm sure the rest are along the same vein. There's not even one measly secret. It's all kissy, kiss, love ya, miss ya, yucky poo."

Raina chuckled. "At least there's nothing explicit where you have to wash your eyes out with bleach."

"I wish there were."

"Po Po, really?"

"Young people aren't the only ones obsessed with getting action in bed. Why do you think there are so many Viagra commercials? I'm not getting any younger. I need to live vicariously through others. It's not like you're giving me any details about your love life."

"What love life? All I do is work and go to my classes." She paused and considered. Her grandma had more of a social life than she did. "Changing subjects here. Thanks for getting me out of Cecelia's office. What did you tell her?"

"Nothing shattering really. Just that Officer Hopper's baby daddy got arrested for running around the park with their three-year-old son." She paused. "They were both naked and another officer had to wrestle him to the ground."

Raina laughed. "She doesn't have any kids."

"So? Oh, and the daddy was slick with body oil. I can't wait to see how long it'll take for this story to get back to the police station. I haven't forgotten how she treated you over Matthew. I'm like the spider in the corner. When the time comes—boo-ya. She's not even going to know what hit her."

Raina's stomach rumbled, and she gobbled down a plump wonton. "I thought that was what Operation Code Red was about."

The aborted plan to throw a stink bomb in the porta potty while Officer Hopper was using it had backfired on the senior citizens. They had driven away from the scene of the crime smelling like week-old gym socks.

Po Po harrumphed and ignored her comment. "I can't believe you don't have Red Bull in your fridge. I thought you young people were all hyped up on caffeine. I have a long night ahead of me. It's my turn to monitor the police scanner."

"Sorry, the only caffeine I have is coffee. What are you doing with a police scanner?"

"I'm the bookie. We're taking bets on the police response time."

"Are the senior citizens of Gold Springs that bored?"

"The mayor and council members are deciding between contracting with the sheriffs or hiring more officers. With only a fourteen-person force, including the chief, the police are understaffed."

"I still don't get why you're monitoring response time."

"Because the bean counters think we don't need either option. You really should pay more attention to the politics."

"No, thanks. Small town politics can be quite deadly."

They ate in silence for several minutes. The chicken broth was so flavorful, her taste buds tap danced their approval.

"Yum. I hope you have leftovers for me tomorrow. Maggie is in a snit so she's not giving me table scraps for a while," Po Po said, lifting a succulent wonton to her mouth.

"What did you do this time?"

"Why do you think it's me? Maybe my best friend just had PMS."

Raina raised an eyebrow. "At her age? She's almost eighty."

Po Po kept eating.

"Please don't tell me this is about me and

Matthew. Po Po, there's nothing for you to worry—"

"Maggie didn't take it too kindly that I called her grandson a poor excuse of a man."

Raina flushed at the thought of Mrs. Louie repeating her grandma's words to Matthew. "Po Po," she said in exasperation.

"I'm just trying to look out for you, but I'll stop."

They went back to eating, but the wontons didn't taste as appetizing as a few minutes ago. How was she to face Matthew and his grandma now? It was all her fault. Po Po rarely fought with her best friend.

"Have you seen Aaron Wheeler at the resort yet?" Po Po asked.

Raina shook her head. "I know he's not a guest, so he must be one of the maintenance or landscape workers. For all I know, he could be the pool boy." She liked the idea of Cecelia stringing her men along with her money. After all, men had been doing the exact same thing to women since the Stone Age.

"I almost forgot this intriguing development. When I opened the door to the closet in Cecelia's office, there was already someone hiding in there. A Chinese woman. I wonder if she's BL's mother. She ran off before I got a chance to question her."

"If she's the mother, she'll be back."

"I'm not quite sure what to do next. I could still try to access the files in Cecelia's offices, but she keeps them locked. So I need to somehow interrupt her in the middle of using them so that she would be distracted enough to leave them open. But with what?"

"How about a fire?"

"I'm not an arsonist."

"I could lob a stink bomb in the office. Toshi Manohar's grandson, Sunil, has been helping me with a new formulation for a super stink bomb. That kid has got talent. He wants to be a chemist. Kimchi sauce mixed with durian fruit juice. The stench is memorable."

Raina stared at Po Po, unsure how to react.

Should she be horrified that her grandma was reliving her childhood or impressed with her inventiveness? Either way, she was just glad her grandma had seemed to fully recover from her bout of depression after her husband's death. "Let me get back to you on this."

10

EASY PEASY

As they headed toward the Venus Café for breakfast the next morning, Raina and Po Po bickered like a pair of doves held too long in a cage. It was nice to have an excuse to spend more time with her grandma.

"I don't understand why you're so reluctant. It'll be fun for me to pretend to check out the resort for my friend's granddaughter," Po Po said, sipping a green tea latte.

Raina shook her head. "With Aaron

working there and the potential murderer hanging around, I don't think so." She had heart palpitations just thinking about her grandma running into either one of them.

"You worry too much. It's not like I'm walking down some dark alley by myself."

"What are you worried about, Raina?" Fanny appeared at their table with a small notepad in her hand. "Is this your grandma?"

Po Po nodded. "Bonnie Wong. And you are?"

"Fanny Lamb. Good morning, Wong Po Po. It's so nice to meet you."

Po Po shot Raina a look as if to say, "see how respectful this girl is." Her grandma would think Ted Bundy was a polite young man if he used her title as Fanny just did in Chinese. Po Po meant maternal grandmother, but the title was also used to show respect for an elderly woman. Just as it was often polite to address someone as if they were a family member by calling them aunt or sister to establish a familial tone in a casual conversation.

Unfortunately it always seemed as if the shopkeepers who followed this practice jacked up the prices once they paused for breath. Apparently, they didn't believe in the family and friends discount.

Before Raina could think of something clever to say to get rid of the foreign exchange student, Po Po and Fanny chatted, asking the usual nosy questions about family and friends as if trying to force a kinship.

Raina ate her eggs and muffin without much input to the conversation. She didn't begrudge Fanny's intrusion into their breakfast. Besides Matthew's grandma, it was rare for Po Po to converse in Cantonese with anyone in Gold Springs. Maybe Fanny would distract her grandma from insisting on undercover work.

She had no idea what would be in Cecelia's files. It wasn't as if the resort owner would document her nefarious activities. The locked cabinet might be just a security measure to keep a nosy person out of her files. Cecelia could be oblivious to what was happening on her property.

Right. As if dancing bears in tutus existed. And how did one explain why someone would hire a private investigator to look into her business practices?

Most people would hand BL to CPS and continue on their merry way, patting themselves on the back for doing all that could be expected given their busy schedules.

But Raina wasn't most people. First, she wasn't particularly busy since it was winter break, and her best friend was out of town. Second, the local police were understaffed, and the mayor would want them to get the baby on a plane to China ASAP. Case closed.

There was no one else. She sneaked a glance at Po Po. Okay, no one else, but Raina and her grandma. She just couldn't stand idly by without at least trying to make sure

BL went back to his proper family. The Liang family couldn't be the right environment for the child if Sui Yuk had to steal a baby.

"Sure, I'd love to help. It sounds like fun," Fanny said. "We can catch the bus after the lunch rush. Say two thirty?"

Po Po nodded. "See you then. And wear a disguise. That's half the fun, you know."

Fanny paused, and a brief frown flickered across her face. "Okay. I'll see what I can dig up." A couple came in, and she left to take their orders.

Raina leaned in and lowered her voice. "What did you tell Fanny?"

Po Po looked offended. "Of course, I didn't tell her any secrets. Then I would have to get rid of her. And I like the respectful young woman. If you'd paid attention instead of sitting here like a stoned pothead, you'd have heard that I wanted a second opinion for my friend's granddaughter."

"I'm not stoned—"

"It's legal, so I'm sure you have your stash like everyone else."

"Po Po! Who are you spending time with?"

Po Po held up her hand, palm out. "No, I'm not judging. Let's get back to the case. We'll drop by Cecelia's office at three fifteen at the latest. Am I good or what? I got myself a body-guard"—she snapped her fingers—"just like that."

Raina sighed. Fanny was more a liability than asset. Aaron Wheeler would snap her like the twig she was. "Just stick close to your field trip buddy."

Po Po saluted. "Aye-aye, Batman."

After dropping Po Po off at her condo, Raina drove to the resort. For the rest of the morning, she couldn't focus on the tasks at hand. She replaced shampoo bottles when she should be replacing soap bars. She pulled out the sheets when she should just remake the bed. To top it off, Raina jumped at shadows and spent far too much time studying all the faces she passed.

By two forty-five, Lucille threw up her hands in disgust and said she was taking a smoking break. "Considering how many times I had to re-do your work today, you should finish up the last two suites."

Raina flushed with guilt. "Sure, that's not a problem. I'm sorry I was distracted. It's the up-coming Christmas dinner with my family. It always sets me on edge."

Lucille's tone became less gruff. "I'll be in the utility room when you're done."

As Raina made her way to Cecelia's office, she considered what she'd blurted out to Lucille. There was some truth to this. She would face her cousins for the first time since they cobbled together a lawsuit contesting their grandfather's will. While Po Po had managed to persuade them to drop the suit, it didn't mean they would welcome her with open arms.

She rubbed the back of her neck, rolling it as she trotted to the lobby area. A Jiggle Me doll to the beloved baby of the family wasn't much of an olive branch. But there wasn't much she could do about it at the moment.

Po Po and Fanny were already behind the large hibiscus shrub outside the lobby of Cecelia's office. Her grandma wore a pair of borrowed bifocals with a wraparound chain. She had stuffed something under her shirt so it looked like she had a dowager's hump the size of a mini backpack. She leaned against a pimp cane with a golden statue of a heavily hung horse. The only thing missing from her disguise was a mole with a long hair growing out of it. Fanny had on a blonde wig that she kept scratching when she didn't think anyone was looking.

Raina didn't know whether to laugh or to groan at their disguises. In the end she settled on giving Fanny a sympathetic smile for her willingness to indulge her grandma. "Thank you," she mouthed.

Po Po grabbed her hand and pressed two small glass bottles in it. "In case you need to make a quick getaway. My super stink bombs." She looked around. "Hurry. Put them away before someone sees them."

Raina obligingly stuffed them in her pocket.

The plan was simple. When they'd called a few minutes ago, the front desk clerk confirmed that Cecelia was working in her office. Mrs. Wong and her granddaughter Fanny would show up, unannounced, to tour the resort. While in the midst of introductions, Po Po would drop a super stink bomb in the office, hence expediting their exit from the room and hopefully leaving everything unlocked. Thereby giving Raina a chance to sneak in and rifle through the contents. Easy peasy. Bada bing, bada boom.

RAINA HID in the shadow of the hibiscus bush. She didn't have to wait long. Within five minutes, there was a mass exodus, with Cecelia

leading them toward the birthing clinic at the north end of the property.

After taking a deep breath, Raina plunged into the office. Breathing through her mouth took some getting used to, but it was worth it when she found both the filing cabinet and the laptop unlocked. She keyed in a general search for Sui Yuk Liang's name on the laptop. While the busy icon whirled on the screen, she opened the filing cabinet and rifled through the folders.

There was an anemic file on Sui Yuk. She cocked her head, studying the folders in front of her. Something didn't look right. She pulled out a nearby folder, noting the thickness of its size. There were the application, emergency contact form, a printout of an email chain that led to the booking of the room, and an itemized billing of services at the birth clinic.

She flipped through the sheets in Sui Yuk's files. Nothing more than an application and an emergency contact form. Someone had removed items from Sui Yuk's file. The application noted that Sui Yuk's baby was due at the beginning of December, but if what Lucille had said about the stillbirth was true, then Sui Yuk delivered late October or early November.

Her shoulders dropped and a heaviness settled on her chest. To carry a baby for that long and to be so close—it's unbearable.

Raina glanced at the doorway and took a deep breath, hoping to clear the emotions whirling in her head. Sweaty gym socks boiled in kimchi hit her with the force of a freight train. She clasped a hand over her nose and mouth. Too late. She'd forgotten about the super stink bomb. Tears streamed from her eyes as she tried to stifle the dying pig noise she was making. She gagged and ran outside.

Bending over, hands on her knees and back against the wall, she sucked in several breaths. Clean, refreshing air. The clock was ticking, but she just couldn't force herself to rush back into the office.

BL's biological mother had to be another guest at the resort at the same time Sui Yuk was here. The due dates for the two women were probably close enough for Sui Yuk to pass off BL as hers. After all, it wasn't like she could go pick up a baby from the hardware store.

Raina took one more deep breath and went back into the office. She checked the laptop, but the search didn't find anything. Surprise. Surprise. She opened the file cabinet again, walking her fingers along the tabs. All the files were at least half an inch thick. She closed the drawer and pulled out the middle cabinet. A quick glance showed files of varying thickness.

She glanced at the clock at the corner of the laptop screen. Fifteen minutes already! Her heart raced in anticipation as she pulled out the last drawer. Since this was only half full, it was easy to see the thin file tucked at the back. Muyang Yao.

She pulled the file out. Bingo! This file

held the same general application and emergency contact form, but nothing else. She checked the due date. November fifth. She snapped photos of the file and shoved it back into the drawer.

As Raina closed the cabinet, her hands shook. Time to hightail it out of there. She had no concrete proof whether Cecelia had anything to do with Sui Yuk Liang's death, but she wasn't going to sit here picking her belly button until the resort owner came back. What she'd found out was enough to get her killed if Cecelia had the temperament.

Footsteps approached the office. "Cece," called out a familiar male voice from the hallway.

Aaron Wheeler!

Raina gasped, a tinny sound that hurt her throat. She dove under the desk and pulled the office chair close until it hid her from view. Half a heartbeat later, Aaron Wheeler's legs came into view in the small gap between the floor and the back panel of the desk. *Don't look down*, Raina prayed, pulling herself into a tight ball.

"What the heck did the woman have for lunch?" Aaron muttered. He came around the desk and opened the closet.

Raina stretched her neck and squinted at the gap between the office chair and desk.

Aaron unzipped Cecelia's purse and pulled out her wallet. He glanced at the door and casually helped himself to forty dollars. He kicked the closet door shut and strode out of the office as if he owned the place.

Raina crawled out from underneath the desk and hurried after him but kept several paces between them, hiding behind corners and bushes. She wasn't ready for a confrontation yet. Whenever she encountered a guest, she pretended to peer into the bushes as if she lost something or drop down on her knees to tie her shoelaces.

As Aaron walked past the pool, a young Arnold Schwarzenegger look-alike strolled out, almost running into him. There were a few seconds of posturing between the two men; neither wanted to yield to the other. The younger man in the fitted shirt had the kind of muscular physique that made some women drool. Raina was surprised Aaron held his ground. The other man could snap him like a Kit Kat bar.

Finally after another tense second, Aaron walked around Mr. Muscles, muttering something that would have gotten her tongue washed with soap. The younger man folded his bulging arms, smirking after Aaron's back.

Raina dodged around Mr. Muscles, but he stepped in front of her, holding out an arm to block her. Aaron made a right and disappeared from view. She rocked back on her heels and crossed her arms.

Mr. Muscles smiled. "Hi, I'm Scotty Bacon. I'm the pool maintenance supervisor." He pointed at the resort logo on her shirt. "You must be new here."

Raina bit inside her cheek to stop the laughter from bubbling out. Ooh la la. Cecelia's pool boy. And with a fancy made-up title too. "I'm Raina Sun. Who is that man? I've seen him around, but he's not very pleasant, is he?"

"Why would you want to have anything to do with Eric Wagner? If you want to get on Cecelia's good side"—he pointed both thumbs at his chest—"I can hook you up."

"Wagner? Is he related to Cecelia?"

Scotty waved dismissively. "He's her ex, but Cecelia owns the place. I guess she must feel sorry for the guy since he can't seem to hold down a job. Every few months, he quits and then comes crawling back. He's the head landscaper, but he doesn't do any work other than skulk about the place. Talk about a loser."

Raina raised an eyebrow. Uh-huh. He should be talking? "What are you doing here? The pool is closed for the winter."

Scotty gave her a look as if she were bubblegum under his shoes. "You have to do maintenance year round. I also maintain the pumps for the two on-site ponds."

"Oh, I didn't know that. So how often do you do this maintenance?"

"Once or twice a week as needed."

Um, right. As if pumps really needed to be checked twice a week. He was here to clear the pipes all right, and she didn't mean the ones in the ground. "Are you two rivals or something?"

"What?"

"You and Eric. I could tell you didn't like each other."

"He keeps throwing empty beer cans in front of my home. What a jerk. Last Saturday he stormed over, accusing me of stealing his firewood. I was this close"—he pinched his thumb and index finger together—"to punching his lights out. I'm not sure how much longer I can do this."

"Wait! You guys are neighbors?"

"Yeah," he said, dragging the word out. "You know that path in the trees behind the

Community Room?" At her nod, he continued. "If you follow it for half a mile, there's a clearing with two trailers in it. Eric and I live there. In separate trailers."

"Does Cecelia live with you?"

"What gives you the idea that Cecelia and I are together? I'm not the type of guy that would cheat on my girlfriend. So, are you busy Friday night?"

"Cecelia is just your landlady?"

Scotty shrugged. "Well, our girl is too good for trailers now. She has this McMansion on the other side of Putah Creek, away from the railroad tracks. Rolling green lawns and the whole works. You'd think she came from old money. To answer your question, yes and no."

"I don't understand."

"That's okay, sweetheart. Just let me do the thinking around here. What about Friday night? I can pick you up in my Escalade."

His chest puffed out as if she was supposed to be impressed with the size of his car. Didn't he know that it was not the size that mattered, but the engine underneath the hood that counted?

"You have an Escalade? Where do you park it?"

"It's Cecelia's rental and I'm borrowing, but there's plenty of room for rocking." He waggled his eyebrows. "If you know what I mean. And we can always go back to my home later."

"You mean the trailer."

"Hey, don't dis the trailer. It's rent free."

"Wow, this is a good gig you have here. I would love to live rent free."

He gave her a half smile and scratched his armpit. "Yeah, I have it good."

Raina smiled. "What time did Eric come over?"

"Come over for what?"

"The firewood."

Scotty shrugged. "I don't know. When I just woke up."

"So eight or nine in the morning?"

His lips curled as if he tasted something

rotten. "Who gets up that early? Around twelve."

Oh boo. Looked like Eric wasn't Sui Yuk's killer. There was no way he had enough time to run her over and return to the resort to argue with Scotty. "What time do you normally wake up for work?"

"Around the same time."

"Wow. You do have it good. I wouldn't have anything to complain about if I were you."

"But things do get old around here, and I don't mean the people. Maybe I need to cut my hours so I can take some classes. It's not like I can be a pool boy forever."

"Pool maintenance supervisor."

"Huh?"

"Never mind. I have to go."

"Wait, what about Friday night?"

Raina walked backwards going back the way she came. "Sorry. I have to wash my hair. Nice meeting you, Scotty."

"With curly hair like that, I'm sure it needs

a lot of maintenance. What about Saturday night?"

She pretended not to hear him and jogged toward Suite Sixteen to finish the cleaning. Things were certainly more than it seemed around here. Now how could she get in touch with Muyang Yao?

11

THAT'S SOME FUNKY PERFUME

Once she couldn't see Scotty anymore, Raina whipped out her cell phone and sent a text to Po Po, warning her about Eric Wagner. While her grandma was able to fight Eric off outside the old bookstore, she had the element of surprise. Things could turn out differently if Po Po ran into Eric again.

She hoped Fanny could protect her grandma with kung fu or something equally as deadly. But she had a feeling the foreign exchange student was more deadly to the ears than body. She had the look of a screamer.

Raina finished up her duties and hustled home for a shower before her dinner date with the Sullivans. Po Po was already waiting for her by the time she got home. A quick glance at her koi clock showed just enough time to relax before she had to leave.

"How did your undercover investigation go?" Raina asked as she headed toward the kitchen to brew a cup of iced coffee. It was late, and the coffee would probably make her too jumpy for an early night, but she needed the boost to sit through dinner with both a drooling blind date and Fanny. "Do you want anything to drink?"

"No, thanks."

Raina pulled out the two stink bombs Po Po had given her and carefully left them on the kitchen counter. They looked innocent enough, a cloudy liquid in the tiny glass vials. But stomping on one of them would clear the room faster than a deluded *American Idol* contestant. It was a running joke in the family as to whether it was really flatulence or a stink bomb when Po Po wanted to avoid a particularly awkward conversation.

"I just want us to touch base before I turn in for the night." Po Po followed Raina into the kitchen. "I didn't want to wait up for you in case your date turns hot and heavy."

Raina snickered. "Right, hot and heavy in front of three other people? I don't think so."

"The two of you can always go out for dessert afterwards." Po Po wiggled her eyebrows. "Wait. Do you have any protection?"

"I have pepper spray."

Po Po went back to the living room and returned with her purse and the cane tucked under her armpits. She dug out a condom and tossed the package to her.

Raina caught the condom with one hand. Extra lubricant for her pleasure. Easy tear packaging. She tucked the condom into her jeans pocket. It was either that or an uncomfortable conversation she never wanted to have with her grandma. What seventy-five-year-old woman walked around with an extra lube condom in her purse?

"Let's get back on topic. What was your impression of things at the birth clinic?" Raina asked.

Po Po handed over her cell phone. "Take a look at the certification and licenses posted next to the doctors' photos."

Raina flipped through the photos with her finger. She frowned as she studied the universities and medical schools from the Philippines and other places she hadn't heard of. "You would think at least one person on the staff would be from California."

"You would think, right?"

"If there was a baby kidnapping, someone on the staff must have helped them."

"If?"

"Something isn't quite right. And I have no idea what, but it involves BL. Until I see the proof, it's all I'm willing to say about this."

"Well, I'm going to say there is a baby kidnapping until it's proven otherwise."

Ah, the heart of the differences in their outlooks in life. Her grandma had already condemned her husband for his philandering ways, while Raina still held hope, albeit a tiny flicker, there was a misunderstanding about Ah Gong's secret family. If only her grandma was willing to expose this skeleton to the rest of the family so it was no longer solely Raina's albatross.

"Well?" Po Po asked.

Raina shook her head. "Sorry. I was gathering cotton candy. What were you saying?"

"What did you find in Cecelia's office?"

Raina told her grandma about the two files she found in Cecelia's office, following Eric, and the conversation with Scotty.

Po Po's eyes widened. "Maybe you should stop working at the resort. I wouldn't want you to run into Eric again."

"Can't. I'm filling in for Sonia. If I leave without notice, she'll lose her job."

"You have protection, right?"

Raina frowned, thinking about the condom. "Pepper spray and my trusty phone."

"You should carry my cane." Po Po twisted it and the cane opened in half to reveal a six-inch blade.

"Wow, that's neat."

Po Po assembled the cane again. "But here's the money-maker." She tapped the metal balls on the horse statuette. "You push down on this and the mouth opens to spray skunk oil at your opponent. I paid extra to get this feature."

Raina burst out laughing at her grandma's proud expression.

"Hey, you never know when this might come in handy. Everyone just thinks I'm a helpless little old lady with my cane," Po Po said.

"Trust me, no one thinks you're a helpless little old lady, and especially not with that pimp cane. They probably think you're some kind of hustler."

Po Po brightened as if pleased with the idea.

"As much as I appreciate the offer, I can't do my work with the cane tucked under my armpits." Raina poured the coffee over a glass of ice cubes. "I'm curious how Eric's number ended up in the diaper bag. It's a good thing BL is out of reach from the crazies at the resort."

"We're digging up more questions than answers. But one thing I can do is go down to the Clerk's Office and see if we can find a birth certificate. I'll take Maggie with me."

"I guess it's no big deal if Matthew knows we're snooping. After all, he is driving us to the Bay Area for the Christmas dinner. It's about time we touch base with him."

"It's going to be okay." Po Po reached across the dining table to pat Raina's hand. "Don't forget, you have a secret weapon." At Raina's confused look, she added, "The Jiggle Me doll for Lila. You are going to walk in there with the most sought-after toy for the baby of the family. It'll do the trick. Why do you think I would risk life and limb to get my hands on the last one at the store?"

Raina blinked at the tears in her eyes and swallowed the lump in her throat. She threw her arms around her grandma, giving the elderly woman a tight hug. A strange wetness seeped onto the bottom of her shirt. She glanced down as a rank odor filled her nostrils.

Po Po jumped up and took off her jacket, flinging it across the room. The smell intensified. "Oh, shoot. I think I broke the other super stink bomb. Quick, let's go to my place. You can shower there."

Raina coughed, trying to swallow the bile rising in her throat. "I can't just let the smell stay in my apartment."

They cracked all the windows. If she were still living in San Francisco, Raina would have hesitated at unattended open windows, but here in Gold Springs, population six thousand, her neighbors often joked about her big city paranoia. She changed her shirt, but she still drove to the condo with all the windows rolled down.

While she showered, she mentally reviewed her wardrobe options. Her choice was limited to a long sleeve blouse with a frou-frou bow around the neck or a tight shirt with a super low neckline. Sometimes she wondered about her grandma's taste. Po Po had picked these up during her last shopping trip. Even with a push-up bra, Raina couldn't imagine showing up to dinner with her belly button winking at everyone. Too bad a pony T-shirt wasn't date worthy.

Dinner at the Sullivans wasn't exactly a date, but Raina didn't want the guy to find out she was a slob until later. She didn't rank high on the dating market, especially with her Afro-like curly black hair and her secret love for all things geeky, but she didn't want to look like expired goods left too long on the shelf. In the end, she settled on the long sleeve blouse with the frou-frou bow around the neck and black jeans. Close enough to her usual wear without seeming like she'd tried too hard.

Raina wrinkled her nose. Her grandma really should stop experimenting with her stink bombs at her condo. A faint funk clung to the air.

At her entrance to the living room, Po Po pinched her nose. "I'm afraid the smell might still be on you. It's the skunk oil. That stuff doesn't just wash off."

Raina pulled the collar of her blouse to her nose and sniffed inside it. Geez, the smell was on her! "I need to cancel. There's no way I can show up smelling like this. No one would want to sit next to me."

"That would be rude. Brenda probably spent the last few hours cooking. You're just going to have to suck it up and go."

Raina stared up at the ceiling as she sighed. She was a good person. She tried to help those in need. Why did her ancestors play practical jokes on her? Did they not want her to meet a decent man?

"I know. How about some perfume?" Po Po grabbed Raina's hand and dragged her to the vanity table in the corner of the master bedroom. "Take your pick, honey."

Raina's gaze swept over the small bottles. All were the freebies given at the department store makeup counter that her aunts and cousins didn't want. Po Po didn't wear perfume either. She kept these little samplers for her experimentations. "It'll take more than perfume to get rid of the lingering odor." The last thing she needed was to smell like a skunk in a rose bath. She picked up a random bottle.

"Not that one." Po Po grabbed the bottle and set it aside. "I replaced it with...something."

Raina eyed the rest of the bottles as if she were expecting a pie in the face. "What are you going to do for the rest of the night?"

"Finish translating the rest of Sui Yuk's

emails." Po Po's lips curled in disgust. "I have a feeling it's going to be more kiss kiss yak. Don't be surprised if you see me walking around with an eye patch tomorrow."

RAINA PULLED up in front of the two-story craftsman bungalow in the cul-de-sac. Candy cane lights lined the driveway. The front yard had a low white picket fence, preventing the inflatable snowman and reindeers from invading the sidewalk. Santa competed with snowflake-hung lights on the roof. If not for the dent on the black pickup parked in the driveway, Raina would have kept right on going. Picture perfection always made her skin crawl and her eye twitch.

Before the doorbell finished its chime, Brenda swung the front door wide open. "Come in."

Raina handed her a bottle of Sauvignon

Blanc. "I wasn't sure what you were serving for dinner, but I hope this will do."

Brenda took the wine and Raina's jacket. "This is perfect. We're having chicken cordon bleu and your cheesy rice pilaf. Love the recipe, by the way." She hung up the jacket in the small closet by the door and led them further into the house.

The living room consisted of exposed overhead beams and wood paneling. A small fire crackled on the right, warming the entire room. The Sullivans had set up a playpen in the far corner. A trimmed Christmas tree with presents underneath winked at them from the family room at the back of the house. Raina wanted to throw herself on the plush rug in front of the fire and call this place home.

Raina hadn't seen the twinkle of inner happiness in her friend's eyes for a while. It warmed her heart to see it there once again.

"Joe and Fanny are still upstairs," Brenda said. "I asked them to give us a few minutes alone because there's someone I want you to meet."

Raina took a deep breath. This was it. Time to meet her date with destiny. She just hoped he still had all his front teeth, unlike some of her previous blind dates.

Brenda grabbed Raina's hand and tugged her to the corner. She flourished her hands in a ta-da gesture in front of the playpen. "Meet the newest addition to our family. We're calling him Johnny. Isn't he a cutie?"

Raina gasped in surprise. BL cooed and pumped his chubby legs in greeting. This had to be a sign from her ancestors.

"Joe and I are foster parents. Yay." Brenda waved her hands in front of her in a mini cheer. "The social worker said his mom abandoned him. Poor baby. So he's a John Doe. Well, the social worker calls him John Liang. We're calling him Johnny."

"Congratulations. I know how much you wanted children, but I didn't know you guys signed up to be foster parents."

"We're on the waiting list to adopt a baby"—she leaned close and whispered—"I thought fostering would be a good way to give Joe some hands-on experience with kids."

"Did the social worker tell you anything else about Johnny?"

"No, why?"

Raina bit her lip. Since the social worker didn't say anything about Eric Wagner aka Aaron Wheeler, should she warn the Sullivans? "Where did you get all this baby gear?"

Brenda blushed. "I bought them a while ago when I thought there was still a chance we could have a baby of our own."

Raina could feel her eyes soften. Poor woman.

Brenda stiffened as if someone yanked a string attached to the top of her head. "Hey, don't give me that look. I don't need your pity."

Raina smoothed her expressive face. "Sorry." Why did she keep doing this when she was around Brenda? At this rate, her friend would stop confiding in her. Time to change the subject. "Did the social worker tell you anything about Johnny's history or anything about his parents?"

"There's not much. Just that he was abandoned at Bullseye."

Fanny bounded down the stairs and came over. "What do you think? Do you like your men drooling and cute? Ha ha. Raina thought you were setting her up."

Raina flushed, wishing a shoe would fly into Fanny's mouth and choke her. "I don't know where you got that idea." Now it was Brenda's turn to give her the pitying look. Geez, she wasn't desperate and dateless... yet.

Fanny wrinkled her nose. She leaned in and sniffed. Her hand flew to her nose, pinching the nostrils closed. "What are you wearing? That's some funky perfume."

A bead of sweat rolled down Raina's back. She closed her eyes, hoping for a hole to open up.

"Would you like to hold Johnny?" Brenda

said, trying to fill in the awkward silence.

Raina nodded, more eager than she realized. When she picked up BL, his chubby fist grabbed one of her curls and stuffed it in his mouth. He stuck his tongue out and batted at his mouth. And just like that she was glad to be here. "Oh, sweetie, I missed you."

Brenda gave her a confused smile. "You've met Johnny before?"

In that moment, Raina made up her mind to warn the Sullivans about Eric Wagner. "Oh, yeah. And boy, do I have a story to tell you about me and this sweetie pie."

Dinner was fabulous, as Raina knew it would be. The chicken cordon bleu was soft, requiring no more than the flick of a fork to slice off the meat. The rice pilaf had just the right amount of cheese and milk for a rich and creamy melt-in-your-mouth taste. But she hid the roasted Brussels sprouts in her napkin when no one was looking. After several minutes of forks clinking and enthusiastic chewing with BL cooing in the background, the Sullivans were ready for dinner conversation.

Brenda sat back and reached for her wineglass. "What's this story about you and Johnny?"

Raina told the Sullivans about what happened at Bullseye with Sui Yuk Liang and Eric Wagner showing up at the old bookstore afterwards. "Please be very careful. I'm sure the social worker wouldn't give away the location of BL, I mean Johnny, but you never know. It's a small town, and you could run into Eric Wagner when you're out and about." She didn't mention anything about the baby kidnapping or the strange business at the resort. That would be too much information.

The Sullivans looked at each other. The kind of look between married couples that held an entire conversation. What Raina wouldn't give to share such a look with someone.

"Thanks for telling us this," Joe finally said. "With Fanny helping at the cafe, maybe

I'll just take the rest of the week off to stay with Johnny."

Fanny's mouth was full at the moment, but her face darkened as if she wanted to protest. She swallowed and studied BL through narrowed eyes. Maybe Fanny thought it was a lark to play at cashiering, but a real commitment to the café was more than she bargained for. Raina smiled to herself at the thought and immediately felt mean-spirited for being judgmental. Having a conscience could be such a downer at times.

Raina was in the middle of telling her friends about the stink bomb incident in her apartment when the doorbell rang. Brenda was still chuckling when she got up, but the frown she came back with chased the light away. Matthew and Officer Hopper followed fast on her heels.

"Sorry to interrupt your dinner, folks," Matthew said. "But we would like to ask the residents in this household some questions relating to a police investigation."

12

IT'S A CURSE

"Mr. Sullivan, is there somewhere we can talk in private?" Officer Hopper asked.

Joe shared a look with Brenda as he stood. "We can talk in the office." He led Officer Hopper down the hallway on the left and they disappeared from view.

"Mrs. Sullivan, could we talk in the kitchen?" Matthew asked.

BL stirred and cried out from the living room. Fanny jumped as if she were prodded by a stick. Brenda hesitated as if she was un-sure whether she should continue to the kitchen or make a beeline to living room. BL cried again.

"Could we talk in the living room?" Brenda went into the living room without waiting for an answer. She picked BL up and walked over to the sofa.

Matthew and Raina followed her out. He studied the Chinese baby and flicked a glance at Raina, silently asking a question about the baby. She gave him a blank stare, and he sighed as if he just got some bad news.

"I would like to talk to Brenda in private," he said.

Raina threw him a look, but knew better than to argue in front of other people. She held out her hands. "Do you want me to hold him for you?"

Brenda shook her head. "Could you warm up his bottle? It's already made up in the re-frigerator."

When Raina poked her head in the kitchen, Fanny, with a worried look, handed her a warmed bottle. Maybe Fanny wasn't so bad after all. When all was said and done, how a person reacted in a crisis said more about her than anything else.

She got back to the living room just in time to hear Brenda say, "Joe must have hit an animal. I wasn't with him at the time." Her friend accepted the bottle with a nod of thanks.

Raina took a couple steps towards the kitchen, then stopped to hunch over her shoes as she undid her laces. Why was he asking about Joe's truck? This couldn't be about a minor traffic violation.

She strained her ears but didn't catch Matthew's next question. When she looked up, both Matthew and Brenda watched her. So much for being sneaky. "Tying my shoes. Just ignore me."

Matthew raised an eyebrow but kept

silent. Brenda glanced at the hall, worry for her husband written all over her face. When Raina entered the kitchen, her shoes squeaked against the laminate wood.

In front of the refrigerator, Fanny whirled around. Her face was smeared with some kind of white cream. She chewed and swallowed. "What do the police want?"

"You're eating?" Raina asked incredulously.

Fanny licked her lips. "I'm a stress eater."

At any other time, Raina would have savored the moment. As it was, she didn't have time for the foreign exchange student. She flipped the lock to the back door. "I'll be back in minute."

"Are you leaving? I wish I could leave, too."

"I'm taking a look at Joe's truck."

Raina rounded the corner of the house to the narrow side yard. The moonlight didn't penetrate this narrow strip of space between the two homes. She pressed the flashlight app on her phone and aimed the weak beam on the ground. As she tugged the latch of the gate, the hair on the back of her neck stiffened. She spun around and gasped at the dark shadow towering over her.

"It's just me," Fanny whispered. "Sorry. I didn't want to stay in the kitchen by myself."

Raina gave her a sharp look, but it was lost in the dark. As she went through the gate, the hair on the top of her head stirred to the beat of Fanny's breaths. Yuck.

There was a large dent on the pickup and some damage to the bumper. In the dim light she couldn't tell if there was blood or other stains. "Do you know what happened?"

"Not really. When Joe came home on Saturday, it was already like this."

"What time was this?"

Fanny shrugged. "After I missed the bus."

"I thought you said Joe had an emergency so he couldn't drive you to Bullseye. What was the emergency?" Brenda hadn't mentioned any health problems, but then people didn't go around blabbing everything to their friends. "Did he back into a pole or something?"

Raina had backed into a pole once in high school, which earned her a bus pass for the rest of the year. Not that the damage on Joe's pickup looked like it came from a pole. The police wouldn't be inspecting the truck unless they thought it was somehow related to Sui Yuk Liang's hit-and-run accident.

"I don't know, but he looked out of it when he came back."

Raina frowned. Joe didn't have the look of a secret addict. "Was he high? Or do you mean he wasn't all there?"

"It wasn't drugs drugs."

"What is that supposed to mean?"

"He takes some kind of medication. I have no idea what. You'll have to ask the Sullivans."

Was it possible Joe could have hit Sui Yuk Liang while under the influence of a medication? Could he be charged like a DUI driver?

Officer Hopper came out the front door. She clicked on a flashlight and swung the beam until it splashed around the pickup. "Hands up where I can see them."

Raina squinted and held a hand over her face. She hated when a bigger light stick showed up at the party. Time to pack it up and go home.

RAINA'S PHONE rang as she stepped through her grandma's front door. It was her mother. She should let it go to voicemail, but Mom would call again every half hour until she answered the phone. Better off just to get the conversation over.

"Hi, Mom," Raina said as she dropped her purse on the kitchen island. She read the note her grandma left on the countertop to let her know she was monitoring the police scanner.

"I spoke with Cassie last night," Mom said. She chattered about Lila and her sister's shopping trip at the mall.

Raina grabbed a fitness magazine from the coffee table and settled on the sofa. There was no such thing as a quick conversation with her mom.

Time was meaningless to a person who never held a job her entire life. She went straight from her parents' house to her marriage with no transition in between. When Dad died ten years ago, Mom was back into her parents' house with her children in tow.

Raina muttered "oh really" and "uh-huh" whenever there was a lull in the conversation while she read an article about the merits of rock climbing. Mom could carry on a conversation all by herself. Once Raina had left to use the restroom, and her mom didn't even notice she was gone.

"Are you mad at Cassie? Why are you refusing to loan your sister some money?" Mom asked.

Raina straightened. It usually took her mom at least twenty minutes to get to the point. "Do you know what she wants the money for? I'm not paying off her credit cards. It's not my problem that she can't control her spending."

"I can understand that you don't want to share your inheritance with your cousins, but this is your sister. You have no idea how much it costs to raise a family in San Francisco."

While Raina could sympathize with Cassie, they could move to a cheaper city or town. "I still don't see how this is my problem."

"It's your duty to help your siblings. It's not like you need all that money for yourself."

Whenever Mom spoke of duty in helping out a family, it invariably meant Raina had to give something up because she had the unfortunate luck of being a first-born. Technically, she was her mom's first child, but her dad's second.

Mom was the youngest and the only girl

in her family. By the time she came along, Ah Gong's shipping business had taken off, which meant she didn't have to work in the warehouses by the port like her six older brothers did. Her childhood was full of rainbows and butterflies where one of her brothers always stepped in to keep the dark clouds away. Her adult life wasn't much different.

"If Cassie had visited Ah Gong more than once when he was in the hospital, he might have left her something," Raina said with a trace of irritation in her voice.

"She was a new mom with a baby. You are single with plenty of free time."

"She's a stay-at-home mom with a nanny. I worked full time with a one-hour commute each way, and yet I managed to visit Ah Gong several times a week. And when he got home, I drove him to every appointment."

"Honey, you need to let it go. You make sacrifices for your family. Now put on your big girl panties, and stop whining."

Raina rubbed her temples. Why did every

conversation with her mom always make her out to be a self-centered brat? "Mom, I need to go. I'll see you in a few days."

"Wait! What about Cassie?"

"I'll think about it." Raina hung up before her mom could finagle the promise out of her. Sure, she would give her sister money to pay off her credit cards—when pigs fly. Her husband was a partner at their Uncle Anthony's law firm. Raina ate more Spam and Ramen on a regular basis than her sister did.

This design to profit from Raina's supposedly newfound wealth would only get worse. Until everyone realized the three million dollars was meant to care for their grandfather's eldest son and mistress, Raina would always get blamed for the division of Ah Gong's wealth. Po Po needed to expose her husband's infidelity to the rest of the family. But what self-respecting woman would rush to let everyone know how she was hoodwinked her entire married life?

WHEN RAINA WOKE the next morning, Po Po was already at her exercise class. She was hoping to catch her grandma to discuss what happened at the Sullivans last night. Apparently retirement kept a person busy. Her grandma's social calendar was miles longer than hers.

Raina swung by the Venus Café to grab a bagel and coffee. Brenda worked the cash register while another woman filled the orders. They exchanged morning pleasantries, but there was no time or privacy to talk about last night's police visit.

The Spanish music was already blaring by the time Raina trudged into the utility room. She nodded at Lucille and started folding towels. Her conversation with her mom left her in a rare mood—somewhere between irritation and guilt. As much as she outwardly denied it, Raina knew she had mommy issues that were probably best hidden in the weak morning light.

The Spanish music stopped, and Raina looked up at the sudden silence. Lucille took a long drag at the cigarette dangling from her fingers, eyeing her the entire time.

"What's going on? You look like a dog ate your breakfast," Lucille said, her voice scratchy and sharp.

Raina shrugged, hoping it would prevent further questions. "Just rolled off the wrong side of the bed."

"I hope you're not going to be as sloppy as yesterday. I'm not redoing your work. Here." Lucille held out a sheet of paper. "This is your half of the work. Go ask Cecelia where she stored the other maid's cart. You're flying solo today."

Raina glanced at the room numbers. "This is not half."

Lucille shrugged as she pushed the maid's cart out the doorway. "I figured the two extra suites should make up for my help yesterday."

Raina glared at her coworker's retreating back. Not only were the extra suites the bigger bungalows, Lucille waited until they finished loading up the maid's cart before mentioning her maiden flight. Geez, the woman should just cackle and fly around with a broomstick between her knees.

As the sliding glass lobby doors whooshed shut behind Raina, a blast of warm air hit her face. She stood for a moment, letting the heat take the chill off her body. The front desk clerk glanced up from the cell phone in her hands, a welcoming smile on her face. When she noticed the resort logo on Raina's shirt, she nodded and returned to her phone.

"Is Cecelia here yet?" Raina asked.

"Ya-huh," the clerk mumbled, dragging her eyes from the small screen. "Are you going there now?" She pulled out a cardboard box from under the counter. "Can you give this to her? It came in yesterday's mail. Thanks." She returned to her phone.

Raina grabbed the package and wondered

if people were just plain ruder these days. At least the clerk said thanks. As she approached the office, tendrils of a rose scent drifted out from the interior. If Cecelia's perfume were visible, Raina imagined it would be a light pink haze with the consistency of cotton candy and the reach of octopus legs. Her eyes itched before she even crossed the threshold.

Cecelia looked up from her laptop. "Good morning, Raina. What can I help you with?"

Raina handed her the package. "Good morning. The front desk clerk asked me to give this to you."

Cecelia frowned at the smudged return address and grabbed a pair of scissors from the cup on her desk.

"Lucille decided we should split up today," Raina said. "Where is the other maid's cart?"

Cecelia glanced at Raina while her hands opened the flap. "It's in the shed to the right of the Community Room."

Raina frowned at the dark interior of the

box. Was something moving inside it? She took a step back.

"What's wrong?" Cecelia asked. A worried look crossed over her face, and she jerked her hands back from the box.

The gap between the flaps widened, and a Pepto Bismal pink balloon expanded until it pushed the flaps apart. The balloon kept growing.

Cecelia's mouth fell opened.

Raina's back brushed against a hard surface. She glanced over her shoulder, surprised she backed up to the doorway.

Pop!

Something slimy oozed down the side of her face. A burnt plastic scent clung to the air, so the whole office smelled like someone left a plastic plate in the microwave too long. Her heart rate sped up. Her hand rose to touch her face. The slime was thick and hot pink. She glanced at Cecelia.

The resort owner's chest heaved as if she were running from a predator. She was covered from head to toe with splatters of the slime. Her bulging wide eyes fixated on the package on her desk.

Raina's gaze traveled to the box. Nestled in the ruins of the pink balloon and a pile of yellow joss paper rested a paper doll in a pool of hot pink slime.

13

JUMP OVER THE FIRE

Raina shivered as if someone had walked over her grave. The hair on her forearms stood at attention. The coarse yellow joss paper was an offering to appease the angry spirit of a dead baby. She prayed whoever sent the package only had a vendetta against Cecelia. *Please don't let this have anything to do with BL.*

"We should call the police," Raina said. Her voice came out sounding like a cartoon mouse.

Cecelia shook as if awakening from a

trance. She smiled, but only one side of her lips twitched like a puppet master forgot to lift the other string. "There's no need for the police to get involved. This is just a practical joke."

"You don't send joss paper as a joke. It's for the dead, and very bad luck in Chinese culture to use it like this." Raina gestured at the package. "This is a curse."

Cecelia grew even paler, but she tried to laugh it off. "I can assure you this is a joke. It's poor taste, but certainly not a curse. Why don't you go home for today? You are clearly rattled."

"What is the return address?"

"It's smudged."

"But you must have an idea who would play this kind of joke on you."

"Probably my ex-husband. He might have walked out on me, but he never got over that I became a millionaire after he left."

Raina frowned. "But Eric isn't Chinese.

How would he know where to even find joss paper?"

Cecilia's head swiveled, and she studied Raina with beady eyes. "You know Eric?"

"No, but I've seen him around the resort."

"Oh," Cecelia said, brushing a clump of slime off her shoulder. "Go home for today. Lucille can finish up on her own."

Raina nodded stiffly and left the office. She didn't believe for a second that Cecelia had no clue who sent the package. While crime could be random, exploding joss paper was not.

Instead of going home, Raina went to her grandma's condo. Po Po took one look at her and told her to wait outside. She disappeared into the kitchen and returned with a stainless steel salad bowl and a plastic trash bag. She set the bowl in front of the threshold, threw in a handful of thin joss paper with gold metallic squares, and lit them. This cleansing ritual had been used by housewives to keep "the dirty stuff" outside the home for centuries.

The gold metallic squares would attract the good will of higher-level gods.

"Jump over the fire," Po Po said.

Raina did as instructed, feeling a sense of calm flow over her at the familiar ritual. Even in the modern world, there was a place for superstition, just as a placebo often had a similar effect on patients.

"Quick," Po Po said as her gaze scanned the hall, "take off your clothes." She held out the plastic bag.

Raina crossed her arms. "What?"

"I don't want pink slime all over my house." Po Po shook the bag. "Just do it before someone comes by."

Raina clenched her jaw. Either she continue to argue with her grandma or drive back to her apartment. Neither option was appealing, but she did want the shirt off ASAP. The cold slime was giving her the heebie-jeebies.

As she whipped her head up and down the hall, she pulled off her jeans and dropped them into the trash bag. She grabbed the edge of her shirt and pulled it over her head. Her hands slipped on the thickening pink slime, trapping her forearms against her face. Yuck.

"Help," Raina said, struggling to free her arms from the tight vise.

Po Po's hands grabbed the back of her shirt and tugged, freeing an elbow. Almost there.

Ding! The elevator whooshed open. Cheerful conversation between an elderly man and his granddaughter drifted over, along with their approaching footsteps.

"Inside," Po Po whispered next to her ear, giving Raina a gentle shove.

Raina stumbled and fell onto the floor. The impact knocked the breath out of her.

"What the—"

"Grandpa, why does she have holes in her underwear?" the little girl asked. "I don't have holes in my underwear. Golly, the underwear is as big as a hat."

Raina groaned, glad the shirt covered her flaming face. Po Po was right. Apparently one never knew when she would be flashing her underwear in public. Why didn't she wear the new panties her grandma had gotten her?

Thirty minutes later, Raina wore a pair of her grandma's silk pajamas and huddled over a cup of steaming coffee on the barstool by the kitchen island. She told her grandma about what happened at the resort. "Someone is out to get Cecelia. Probably BL's mother."

"It could be another matter entirely," Po Po said. "Cecelia might have all kinds of enemies, for all we know."

"What did you find out in Sui Yuk Liang's emails?"

Her grandma averted her gaze, staring out the window at the overcast sky. "I didn't quite get to it last night."

"Po Po."

"Don't use that tone on me. The emails are boring, and I already did half of them. You should finish them. Just think of it as practice."

"Fine," Raina said. It took all of her

willpower to stop her eyes from rolling to the back of her head.

"You know I'm more of a doer than a thinker."

"Uh-huh," Raina said slowly. She rubbed her hands on the leg of her silk pajama bottoms. This moment was as good as any. The upcoming Christmas dinner would be the perfect time to reveal Ah Gong's other family. Her grandma should understand they couldn't keep it a secret forever.

Po Po snapped her fingers. "Earth to Rainy. I said there was no birth certificate for Muyang Yao's baby, but there was one for Sui Yuk Liang's baby."

Raina blinked as her grandma's words sparked a light bulb in her head. "So this is why the Chinese woman is snooping around Cecelia's office. She couldn't very well ask the police to return BL to her."

"How do we even know she is BL's mother? She could be delusional or suffering from postpartum like Matthew said."

"There's only one way to know for sure—a DNA test."

"And where would we get a sample of BL?"

"You're not going to believe this." Raina told her grandma about the cutie pie at the Sullivans and the police visit from the night before. "They must have called around the body shops to see if anyone brought in a damaged vehicle."

"What did Joe tell the police?"

"I don't know. I haven't had a chance to talk to the Sullivans. But getting a sample from BL shouldn't be a problem."

Po Po stood. "What are we waiting for? We can't let an innocent man take the fall for the murder. Let's grab a pastry from the Venus Café to go with that coffee you're drinking."

"Slow down. We don't know if Joe is even accused of a crime yet." Raina held out her mug. "Besides, I can't bring my own coffee to a cafe."

"I don't see why not."

"Matthew is on the police force. He'll do the right thing."

"I'm not so sure. Since he is stupid enough to let you go, I have no faith in his ability to see things in shades of gray."

THEY HOPPED into Raina's car for the short drive to the café. Normally they would have walked, except the swollen clouds threatened a heavy rain. Raina turned off the radio; the false cheer of the Christmas music reminded her that the countdown to D-day was around the corner.

"What good is a sample from BL if we don't have a sample from Muyang Yao?" Po Po asked. "I have a feeling she has something to do with the curse. We need to smoke her out."

"One thing at a time," Raina said. "Muyang would continue to circle around Cecelia if she believes the resort owner stole her baby."

"Whoever put the curse together probably couldn't find black dog blood and so had to improvise with pink slime. Without the blood, the curse is nothing more than window dressing. Too bad Chinatown is so far away. You can find anything in Chinatown if you know where to look."

Raina slid a sideways glance at her grandma. Sometimes she had no idea if Po Po was serious or just making conversation. "I don't see the mousy woman being so aggressive. She was practically weeping from fright in Cecilia's closet."

"Honey, if this woman is BL's biological mother like we suspected, she's a mother bear waiting for her chance to strike. And why are we calling her 'woman'? I thought her name was Muyang Yao."

"We don't know this—"

Po Po waved dismissively. "Pfff. Semantics. She needs a name, and Muyang Yao is as good as any."

"And what happens if Muyang Yao is another person, and we're focusing our energies on the mousy woman?"

"We'll cross that bridge when we get to it."

"If Muyang is dangerous, we shouldn't bait the bear."

"She's no match for the two of us."

Raina clicked on the right turn signal. *Unless she happens to run people over like bowling pins.* "I'm open to suggestions."

"How would I know? I'm the ideas person, Batman. You're the details person of this team. Go figure it out and let me know what I need to do."

Raina rolled her eyes. Geez, she'd like to be the ideas person too if it meant just showing up for the party. "I guess we can send her an invite."

"We don't even know where she is staying."

"We could make her come to us. Set a trap and then spring it like you said."

"You mean like a billboard or something?"

"Why not? We can buy an ad space in the

town newspaper saying we have Sui Yuk Liang's baby and we're looking for information on his mother. It's not like the hit-and-run information is public knowledge yet."

"Matthew is going to flip when he sees the ad," Po Po said, her eyes gleaming with glee. "Your friend Eden isn't going to like this either. When is she supposed to be back in town?"

"Saturday. And by that time BL would be on a plane to China. Whether or not he would be heading to his biological family is up to us. So Eden's irritation at being excluded from insider information on a story is the least of my worries."

"But what about Matthew?"

"What about him? I'm not interfering with his murder investigation. I already told him I'm looking into the baby's parentage."

Po Po's smile widened. "Right-de-o."

Raina checked the time on her dashboard. "The newspaper office closes in fifteen minutes." She made a U-turn, heading north on A Street.

"Muyang is going to want to meet at a public place," Po Po said.

"How about the Senior Center? It's your turf. And she might let her guard down if she thinks she's dealing with a helpless elderly woman."

Po Po straightened. "Now wait just one min—"

"I said think. I didn't say is. You're the least helpless person I know. But just play your part, okay?"

Po Po harrumphed. "I'm going to need a disguise."

A few minutes later, Po Po paid for the half-page spread and they were back in the car and on their way to the Venus Cafe again. There was a sign posted on the door of the Venus Cafe. "Open until one o'clock on Christmas Eve. Closed Christmas Day." They got in line.

"We might as well have an early dinner

since we're here already," Po Po said, studying the specials written on the small chalkboard next to the counter. "What do you think— meatballs or French dip?"

"Want to do take-out? I'll get myself something from Thai Chili."

"Sure. What did Matthew say when you told him Aaron Wheeler is actually Eric Wagner?"

"He doesn't know. I don't feel comfortable just calling him like I used to." Raina squirmed under her grandma's steady gaze. "Things are just weird between us."

Po Po muttered under her breath, "I'm going to have to teach that boy a lesson."

"No, Matthew isn't doing anything. You don't spend most of your life thinking you'll end up with someone and then pretend like nothing happened. I can't compartmentalize it yet."

"I'm sorry you can't make a clean break."

Raina shrugged. A clean break between them would be akin to cutting off an arm or leg. It just wasn't going to happen any time soon. "I'm wondering if I should leave Gold Springs."

"Are you going to let a man chase you out of town? Come on, girl. Chin up and shut up."

Raina smiled at the gruffness in her grandma's voice. "Thanks for the tough love. I'm not leaving, but the idea does have its appeal."

"Good. If anyone has to leave, it should be him. You know someday he's going to be crawling back because we all know you're the best thing since sliced salami and pickles."

"And when he does"—Raina struck out a fist—"ka-pow. He can eat my five-knuckle sandwich."

When they got to the counter, Raina was surprised to see Joe working behind the cash register.

"Where is Fanny?" Raina asked. "I thought she was supposed to help out."

"She's in the kitchen assembling take-out orders." He paused, frowning. "Or maybe she went to pick up supplies?" He shrugged. "She's somewhere helping. I'm sure glad we have the extra set of hands."

"Who is watching the baby? Is he here?" Raina asked.

"Oh, I would love to see him," Po Po said.

"Sorry, ladies, but he's home with my mom. She drove in early this morning and is staying through the New Year to help out with the baby."

Raina shared a look with her grandma. The authorities would expedite the process to get BL back to the Liang family. There was no way he would stay with the Sullivans until New Year's. She didn't know Joe well enough to ask about his interview with the police. "Where's Brenda?"

"She's out picking up supplies," Joe said.

Po Po placed her order, and they made their way to the leather armchairs in front of the fireplace. As Raina called in her order to the Thai restaurant next door, the bell on the front door jingled.

"What are they doing here?" Po Po whispered.

Raina followed her grandma's gaze to the pair coming into the cafe. Matthew and Officer Hopper. Both of them looked grim and serious. This wouldn't be good news. But for whom? Officer Hopper got in line behind the last customer. Matthew strolled over to the fireplace at the same time Fanny came out from the kitchen with Po Po's take-out order.

Fanny's eyes lit up like a fireworks display at the sight of Matthew. Raina almost felt sorry for the girl, but then realized that she might have looked just as pathetic herself until she'd wised up.

"Hi, Matthew. Do you want to get something to eat?" Fanny said, holding the take-out bag to Raina. "Nice outfit."

Raina flushed as she grabbed the bag. So silk Chinese pajamas weren't exactly fashionable. It wasn't like she was at a ball.

"No, thanks," he replied. "Raina, I need to

talk to you. Can you come outside with me for a few minutes?"

She handed the takeout bag to her grandma. "Don't worry," she whispered into Po Po's ear, "no one is bringing sexy back."

14

A WARNING

Raina followed Matthew outside and watched as he walked over to Joe's black pickup truck. In the afternoon light, the damages to the hood and bumper were even more noticeable than the night before. She rubbed her hands on her thighs.

Matthew gestured for her to come over. "Do you know what happened to his truck?"

Raina shook her head as a sense of foreboding settled into her stomach. *Please let Joe hit a deer or something.* "What's going on? Why are you so interested in the Sullivans?"

"This is just routine. We're checking out all the vehicles that have damages," Matthew said. "Don't worry. A neighbor saw Joe sleeping in the living room at the time of the accident."

Raina smiled. "That's great news. I knew the Sullivans wouldn't have anything to do with Sui Yuk Liang's death."

"The neighbor didn't notice the truck in the driveway."

Raina's smile slipped. "It was probably in the garage."

"You could be right." Matthew's expression told her he didn't believe the words coming out of his mouth either.

"What about the threatening note? And there's Eric Wagner, Cecelia's ex-husband, pretending to be Aaron Wheeler." She told him about her conversation with Scotty Bacon and the exploding pink slime.

Matthew scribbled down the information

in his notebook. The furrow between his eyebrows could have cracked walnuts. "We've already notified the feds, and an agent will be
here to take over the case. If all goes smoothly,
Baby Liang will be on a plane in a day or two."

Raina's heart skipped a beat and then sped
up. She took a deep breath to calm herself.
"This is so wrong, Matthew. And you know it.
Everyone just wants BL to return to China.
What happened to justice? What about doing
what's right?"

"The baby is not going to know any
different."

"How can you say that? This could impact
BL's entire future. What if the father starts to
suspect this baby is not his son? How would
the father treat him then?"

Matthew rubbed the back of his neck. "It's
not my job to play God. The mayor and the
chief—"

"What if the father abandons him in an
orphanage? Don't forget, you can only have
one child in China. If the father remarries, his

new wife might not want a child that isn't even her husband's."

He averted his gaze and studied the gravel ground for several seconds. "Since he can afford to send his wife here, I'm sure he's wealthy enough to get the exemption to have another child."

"You're not getting it, Matthew," she whispered. "I have to see this through. I can't let fate decide this poor baby's path. I could never live with myself if there was something I could have done, but didn't."

"I swear, Rainy, if you interfere with my investigation—"

"What if Sui Yuk Liang's death is not the end of this? What if whoever killed Sui Yuk goes after BL—"

"How would the killer know where to find the baby—"

"Aha!" Raina pointed a finger at his chest. "So you do believe I'm onto something."

He sighed loudly as he ran his hand through his black hair. "Do you want to get hurt again? Or are you just doing this to get my attention?"

Raina recoiled as if he struck her. "I'm surprised your swollen head hasn't burst yet. This is not about you. We're just friends. Friends. What I need is for you to do your job."

"How do you know I'm not? There are some things I can't tell a civilian."

Tears burned in the back of Raina's eyes and she blinked them away. Had he always been a jerk? How could she be so blind? She swallowed at the knot in her throat. He didn't deserve her tears. She could cry later. "So doing your job involves shoving an innocent baby—"

"I'm not the monster you make me out to be. Just have a little faith that everything will work out without your interference. It's the season for miracles."

Raina snorted. "Like you would know anything about faith or miracles. You're a man who still has daddy issues—"

"Leave my dad out of this—"

"And I'm not your mom. You come at me with your fists, and my skillet is going to connect with that pea brain—"

Matthew reached up to grab her face with both hands and kissed her. A deep, thorough kiss that curled her toes. His arms wrapped around her, pulling her close. His clean citrus and sage scent overwhelmed her senses and caused her knees to weaken.

Raina shook as if she were standing in a thunderstorm. She shoved him away, slapped him, and swiped at her swollen lips. Her chest heaved, and her face felt hot and tight as if she just ran in a race. What was he doing?

His nostrils flared as if he also ran the same race but was chasing her instead. His reddened cheek was like a beacon against his pale face. "I'm sorry. I don't know what came over me."

Someone coughed from behind them and broke the spell. She hastily stepped aside. Po Po and Fanny watched them, one with concern and the other with irritation. How long had they been standing there? And how much had they heard?

Raina somehow managed to drift closer to her grandma and used the awkward silence to pretend to fix her curly hair.

Po Po snagged her arm. "What do you think you're doing?" she whispered.

Raina glanced at Matthew and then back at her grandma. "That's the problem. I wasn't thinking," she whispered back.

"Stop listening to those hormones. You're not a teenager anymore."

Raina flushed even redder. This was the source of her problem. Matthew was her first. Her body responded on autopilot whenever she got a whiff of his scent. She either had to cut off her nose or dunk him in skunk oil. "Just give me the take-out bag."

Matthew recovered faster than Raina did. He pulled out his cell phone and snapped photos of Joe's truck. He smiled at Fanny as if Raina were nothing more than a garden gnome, which looked ridiculous with the red handprint on his face. "Fanny, when did you first notice the damage to the truck?"

"I have no idea. It was like that when I got back from Bullseye on Saturday." Fanny averted her gaze as if she was embarrassed for him.

"You didn't see the riot at Bullseye?" Po Po lowered her voice into a fake whisper, "I heard the police Tased a couple of people."

Matthew cleared his throat. "About that riot. Wong Po Po, I heard that a little old Chinese woman and her curly haired granddaughter instigated it by snatching a Jiggle Me doll from another customer."

Po Po straightened and gave him a vague smile. A picture-perfect addled old lady. "Rainy, my blood sugar is getting too low. I need to eat something."

Raina shoved her car key and the takeout bag toward her grandma. "Why don't you take care of your business in the car? I'll be there in a sec." She wasn't going to miss this conversation between Matthew and Fanny because of a fake blood sugar problem.

Fanny reached out to steady Po Po. "Do you need help to the car?"

Matthew's eyes glinted in amusement. "Raina can help her feeble grandma, right?"

Raina gave her grandma a significant look. "Po Po, do you feel faint right now?"

Po Po rested the back of a hand on her forehead. "Yes, everything is spinning."

Raina pulled out a piece of bread from the take-out bag and pushed it toward her grandma. "Here, munch on this."

The corners of Matthew's lips twitched. Po Po wasn't fooling anyone.

"Where was Brenda at the time?" he asked.

Fanny looked first at Matthew and then at Raina, ignoring the question. "Are you two... dating?"

"No," Raina said.

"No," Matthew said just as quickly.

"Why were you kissing?" Fanny said.

"We weren't kissing," Raina said with a straight face, focusing on the foreign exchange student so she wouldn't see her grandma's eye roll.

Fanny crossed her arms. "Looked like kissing to me." A deep flush rose from Fanny's throat to her cheeks in a patchwork of pink and white spots like the growth on a petri dish. "Thanks a lot for making me look like a fool."

"We're not together anymore," Raina said.

Fanny slid a sideways glance at Matthew. "No one told me there would be a baby. Then Joe's mom showed up this morning with a suitcase. Now all this trouble with the police." Her voice cracked. "I can't believe this is happening to me."

Raina felt for the foreign exchange student. There was nothing worse than tangling with the law while studying abroad. She shared a look with her grandma.

Po Po raised an eyebrow as if to say it was her call.

Raina tipped her chin. It wasn't her call to make.

Po Po patted Fanny's shoulder. "Do you need a place to stay? I have a spare bedroom that you can use until you find another place."

Fanny gave her grandma a trembling smile. "I don't want to impose. I made the choice to stay with the Sullivans so I have to deal with this. Don't worry. I'll figure something out."

"It's not a problem. If my Rainy was in a similar situation, I hope a nice person would step up to help out," Po Po said.

Fanny twisted the hem of her shirt. "The Sullivans are good people. I don't want them to think I'm abandoning them."

"It might be helpful for you to move out," Raina said. "It's one less thing for the Sullivans to worry about."

"Alright, you've convinced me. Thank you," Fanny said.

A tow truck rattled around the corner and pulled into the parking lot. It looked like the

Sullivans' problems were only just beginning. As the tow truck driver hitched up Joe's truck, Fanny ran back inside the café. Matthew followed after her, pulling a bunch of paperwork out from his back pocket.

Raina felt as if Atlas bounced his burden on her stomach. She whispered to her grandma, "Let's go. I don't want to stay and watch this."

Po Po was unusually quiet during the short drive to Raina's apartment. Her grandma was mulling over something and wasn't ready to share yet, which was fine by her. She wasn't in the mood to talk either.

Raina inserted her key and opened the front door. She poked her head inside and sniffed cautiously. The air was a little stale, but not pungent or foul. She stepped inside and took another sniff. Not bad. A little more airing and it would be fine by the time she went to bed.

Po Po threw her beach-sized purse on the sofa and plopped down next to it, grabbing the remote. "I'm beat. Give me a minute, and I'll help you set the table."

Raina dropped her purse on the side table. "Can't we skip the place setting..." She tilted her head, studying the pile of mismatched socks at the foot of her bookshelf. Wasn't the yellow sock closer to the bottom of the pile before?

She'd always been a piler: mail, books, or clothes. As long as it was stackable, she made little molehills in her living space that made her mom's eye twitch. It could be one of the reasons she did it, but it was probably her need for a little chaos when everything else was so orderly in her previous life as an engineer. Unfortunately, the habit stuck.

Her gaze flicked to the dining nook and the hair on the back of her neck stiffened. The pile of mail on the new-to-me dining room table was too neatly stacked to be her handiwork. Someone had broken into her apartment last night and rifled through her things.

Raina cocked her head, listening to see if

there was someone in the bedroom. But all she could hear was the noise from the TV. "Someone broke into my apartment," she yelled. She didn't fancy coming face-to-face with an intruder.

Po Po turned down the volume. "Why are you screaming?"

"I said—"

"I heard you the first time," Po Po said, grabbing her pimp cane in an attempt to rush into the bedroom.

Raina stuck out her arm, blocking her grandma. "Oh no, you don't. Follow me." She grabbed the tennis racket leaning against her bookshelf. It wasn't much, but it was better than nothing.

They rushed into the bedroom, making enough noise to scare the bejesuses out of a three-year-old. The room was empty. And freezing. The curtains danced as if possessed, which shouldn't have been the case from the small crack she'd left open the night before. On the floor, broken glass glittered and winked on the beige carpet. A rock the size of her fist slept on her pillow like Goldilocks.

Raina stepped around the sharper fragments of glass and opened the curtains. The broken window was closed. She tilted her head, studying the view.

"What is it?" Po Po asked from the doorway.

Raina pointed at the window. "My bug screen is missing."

"The rock must have knocked it off."

Raina stepped up to the sill, careful of the glass, and peered out. The bug screen lay below her window, perfectly intact. She shuddered at the sight as if a spider were crawling down the back of her neck.

"Honey?" Po Po called out.

She looked at her grandma. Her voice was a pitch higher than usual when she answered. "The intruder removed the bug screen and came in through the unlocked window. He snooped around, and when he left, he closed the window and threw a rock through it."

"In frustration? Maybe he didn't find what he was looking for. It's not like you have money under your mattress."

Raina shook her head. "I think this is a warning."

15

PIGS COULD FLY

Raina went back to the living room and grabbed her cordless phone. By the time Officer Hopper showed up at her front door, she'd gone through her belongings. Nothing was missing.

"Not a single thing? Are you sure?" Officer Hopper asked, her pen poised over her clipboard.

Raina nodded. "Yes, I'm sure."

"What about enemies? Or a friend who likes practical jokes?"

"No."

"Are you doing something that you shouldn't be doing? Like poking your nose in police business?"

Raina stiffened. While she didn't expect warm and fuzzy feelings from a previous romantic rival, she did expect professionalism. It was none of the officer's business whether or not Raina was investigating anything. "No."

Officer Hopper tapped on the bottom of the form. "Sign here. You can get a copy of the police report in two business days."

"Wait! Aren't you going to dust for fingerprints? Or see if you can get a hair or something for a DNA test?"

Officer Hopper placed a hand on her jutting hip. "You expect me to get a CSI team out here because someone threw a rock at your window?"

"What about the broken glass?"

Officer Hopper glanced at it. "Make sure you're wearing shoes when you're vacuuming."

"Aren't you going to take some photos?"

"It's pretty clear the rock came from outside the apartment. The glass placement on the floor doesn't require photo documentation. I'll talk to your neighbors. Maybe someone heard or saw something."

Raina bit back a snarky comment and signed the form. After Officer Hopper left, Raina called her landlady, who said she would send someone over the next morning. When she hung up, she collapsed onto her sofa.

"Is someone coming to fix your window?" Po Po asked.

"The landlady said she'd try to get someone, but I'm not expecting any miracles."

Po Po pulled out her cell phone. "Let me see if I can find someone."

Raina left her grandma tapping on her smarty-pants phone. She brought out the plates and emptied the take-out cartons. Her grandma always insisted upon eating off of real plates as if it made takeout seem homemade.

She should clean up her bedroom, but there was time for that later. Right now she needed to bustle around the kitchen until her insides stopped jiggling like the doll she'd wrapped up for her niece.

The shrimp pad Thai noodles blurred, and a drop of tear splattered across the plate. Someone had gone through her underwear drawer. The thought made her vulnerable somehow in a way that personal danger never did. Her cozy little apartment had always been her safe haven. Impenetrable to whatever was happening on the outside. But someone had purposefully made sure she knew her apartment was no longer safe.

"I can't get anyone either," Po Po said, stepping into the kitchen. "Hey, you okay?"

Raina wiped the tears off her cheek. "I want to smash the nose of whoever did this. You don't mess with someone's home. That's sacred."

Po Po wrapped her skinny arms around Raina's shoulders. "And we'll put a stink bomb in their home in retaliation. I have an ultimate stink bomb formulation that I haven't tried yet. We can test it on the intruder's home."

Raina squeezed her grandma's arm and gave her a wobbly smile. "You ready for dinner?"

For the next few minutes they ate in silence. It had been a long day, and Raina was happy to turn her brain off for a moment.

Knock, knock!

She glanced at her grandma. "I thought you couldn't get anyone."

"Maybe the landlady had better luck than me," Po Po said.

Raina squinted through the peephole. Matthew. What did he want? She opened the door to tell him to go home, but stopped at the sight of a paper-wrapped window leaning against his leg.

Matthew handed her a tool bag and bent down to pick up the window, and she stepped aside to let him in. He headed straight into her bedroom with neither one of them exchanging a word. She closed the door and followed behind him.

Po Po's head turned and followed his progress. She swung her head back around at the sound of Raina's footsteps. "Did you call him?" she whispered.

Raina shook her head. "I thought maybe you did," she whispered back.

"Not me."

Po Po shrugged and returned to her dinner. She pulled out her cell phone, and her fingers flew across the screen.

Raina stepped inside the bedroom and handed him the tool bag. "Do you need any help?"

Matthew removed the wrapping around the window. "No, I'm fine."

"Not that I don't appreciate you being my knight in shining armor, but how did you know?"

"I recognized the address over the police radio. I called Donna for the details."

"And you got the dimensions of the window from her as well?"

"I got that from Joanna Hopper."

Raina blinked rapidly at the pressure behind her eyelids. She wanted to fly into his arms and sob on his shoulders. "Do you want me to make you something to eat?"

Matthew shook his head as he removed the casing. "Do you have time to talk?"

Raina sighed audibly. He wanted to talk now? Geez, talk about perfect timing. "What is it this time? It's not me, but you that's the problem. I'm too good or not good enough. Which is it?"

"I'm sorry about the kiss. It's what we used to do before." He grimaced. "I guess I'm having a hard time letting go, too."

Raina snorted, unladylike and ugly to hide her bubbling anger. "We should start seeing other people. Apparently, what we're doing is not enough."

"Do you have someone in mind?"

Matthew asked, almost lazily as if he didn't really care about her answer.

Raina thought about the warm voice of the stranger who called a few days ago asking for a date. All it would take was a phone call to her uncle to track him down. She shook her head. She was responding with her emotions again.

"Well, maybe you'll meet someone soon," Matthew said generously. "Do you want me to stay here with you tonight? I can sleep on the sofa."

"No, thanks. Not that I'm unappreciative"—she gestured at the window and tools—"but you need to let it go. No more boyfriend to the rescue. I could have handled this perfectly on my own."

"Oh, really?" he said, his voice thick with sarcasm. "You tore a ligament on your finger the last time you picked up a hammer."

"You're doing it again," Raina said through gritted teeth. "You're trying to reel me in."

"I'm just being a good friend and trying to help you out."

Raina pressed her lips into a tight line. She didn't want to say something she would regret later. But the glimmer was starting to wear off. Matthew was as manipulative as his mother, and he didn't even know it.

MATTHEW INSTALLED the new window and left. Raina was upset and didn't bother hiding it. He probably assumed it was for the broken window. There wasn't much left to say between them that hadn't been said before.

Po Po helped clean up the bedroom and tried to convince Raina to move into her condo for a while. With Fanny in the guest room, Raina would have to either sleep on the sofa or share her grandma's bed. She wasn't desperate enough for either option yet.

After everyone left, Raina made a cup of chamomile tea and streamed *Big Bang Theory* with half an eye on the ticking koi clock above her TV. Everything was back to normal, but she felt restless. Her skin was too tight, and she wanted to scratch something.

She glanced at the clock again. Half past eight. Too early for bed, but too late for going out. Other than the movie theater, Gold Springs shut down by nine. She crossed the room and took down the clock. The gilded koi fishes swimming around the dial was really too fancy for her apartment. She shoved it into the junk drawer in the kitchen.

Raina trudged into the bedroom to check her window. It was locked...just like ten minutes ago. Why would the intruder want to warn her? Because the person felt threatened by something she had in her possession. She turned to survey the room. There was the threatening note, but what sane person would withhold it from the police? The only other thing she took from Sui Yuk Liang's room was photos.

Her eyes widened. The emails! She hadn't

forgotten about them, but given her grandma's lack of interest, Raina didn't feel any urgency to look them over. Tonight was as good a time as any to get the translations done.

The work was laborious, requiring alternating searches between the laptop and the Chinese-English dictionary. Unlike most languages, written Chinese didn't have a phonetic alphabet. Learning the characters relied heavily on brute memorization. A literate person would have memorized four thousand words in China. The last time Raina checked, she was illiterate, having only memorized sixteen hundred words.

Two hours and all she got was kissy kiss stuff befitting a high school romance. Raina flexed her hands to keep them from cramping. She yawned and lazily scanned the first of the last four emails, not bothering to look up the unfamiliar words.

Baby kicking blah stomach. Sui Yuk probably meant the baby was kicking hard in her stomach.

Can't wait blah baby. Blah blah for the best. The husband probably can't wait to hold or see the baby. What was for the best? *Tai Tai left for blah blah. I can come for blah blah.*

Raina jerked awake, knocking the dictionary off the dining room table. Whoa! Tai Tai was the formal title for a first wife. Sui Yuk's "husband" was married to someone else. This made Sui Yuk...a concubine.

She was surprised, but at the same time wasn't. While polygamy was no longer legal in China, it didn't mean it wasn't practiced, especially among the wealthy. It wasn't uncommon for foreign businessmen to have a second wife and child in China.

Raina could almost hear her ancestors' laughter. It was serendipity her grandma got bored with the email translations. Po Po would flip if she knew Sui Yuk was a concubine. While her grandma was outwardly fine, Ah Gong's second family in China was like a pus-filled sore waiting to erupt.

She groaned. Once again, she was caught

between two hard places. If she kept quiet, Po Po would be upset when she found out. But if this information had nothing to do with the investigation, why set herself up for an argument with her grandma? This could blow over by itself.

And pigs could fly.

Why didn't someone just buy a raincoat?

16
—

OVER MY DEAD BODY

When the alarm clock rang the next morning, Raina was more than ready to get up. It had been a sleepless night of tossing and checking the bedroom window. The broken window was meant to scare her, and it worked, it also made her angry. It was time to put the squeeze on Cecelia to find out what she knew about BL.

Raina parked at the curb in front of the Venus Café again. As much as she loved the food at the Venus Cafe, her taste buds were starting to protest at the frequency of eating at her favorite restaurant. But it didn't seem right to poke around asking nosy questions without at least being a patron. Ignoring the posted sign, she pulled the front door.

It was locked.

The lights were out. Raina framed her hands around her face but didn't see any movement inside. She stepped back, glancing at the sign. It wasn't the Christmas schedule posted yesterday.

CLOSED UNTIL FURTHER NOTICE

This couldn't be good news. She needed to get in touch with the Sullivans ASAP.

The morning went as expected with Lucille making snide remarks about Raina's laziness and sloppiness. When Lucille announced a smoking break, Raina wanted to shove two packs of cigarettes at her coworker to shut her up.

Raina trotted toward the office, keeping an eye out for Eric Wagner. Outside the lobby doors, the fine hairs on the back of her neck stiffened. She studied the shrubs and trees in front of her. She'd hidden there herself a few days before. A cold wind rustled the leaves. Raina shivered, but she couldn't see anyone.

She knocked on the doorframe of Cecelia's office. "Good morning. How are you doing?"

The office had been cleaned, leaving no hint of an exploding pink slime package. Cecelia leafed through a pile of invoices in front of her computer. Her graying brown hair was pulled into a tight ballerina bun, so that her manly features and wrinkles were exposed in their full glory to the morning sun. While she exuded vigorous health when she was in motion, she seemed shrunken somehow with her reading glasses perched on the tip of her nose and furrows in her brow.

"Good. Can I help you with something?" Cecelia removed her glasses, twirling them by the temples in a casual manner.

"Do you still think it is Eric who sent the package? With the joss paper, I would think it is from a Chinese person. Pissed anyone off recently?" Raina smiled to take the bite off her question. "How about the person who killed Sui Yuk Liang?"

Cecelia licked her lips and said carefully, "My, you have an active imagination. Sui Yuk Liang died in an unfortunate accident." She glanced at the clock. "Isn't this awfully early to be on break?"

"Probably, but Lucille is calling the shots. If you have problems with the break schedule, you should talk to her about it. Do you think Muyang Yao sent you the package?"

"Did you run across her name on one of the guest lists? Lucille should do a better job at ensuring our guests' privacy." Cecelia reached for her phone. "I'm sorry, but I have to make this urgent phone call."

"You ever find out what happened to Sui Yuk Liang's baby?"

Cecelia set the phone down and studied her through narrowed eyes for a long moment. "Curiosity is only endearing in a young child. It has a habit of getting an adult in trouble. Watch yourself."

Raina shifted her weight to her other foot, humming birds bouncing around in her stomach. "Are you threatening me?"

"Ooh, I'm the big bad wolf. Now get back to work."

"Were you able to find somebody to sub for me tomorrow?"

"Lucille's cousin is willing to work Christmas. I'm surprised you don't want the extra pay."

Raina pushed the maid's cart back to the utility room for more toilet paper. She wasn't sure what to make of Cecelia's comments. She was almost sure the resort owner had something to do with the kidnapping of Muyang's baby. But she had no proof and neither did whoever sent her the curse.

Lucille wasn't in the utility room. At the rate she had been taking these smoking breaks, the woman's lungs had to be blacker than Santa's—

Thunk!

Raina jerked her head at the noise coming from the linen closet on the far end of the room. Was someone inside? What if it was Eric waiting to waylay her? Or what if it was Lucille? The door swung opened, and the murmur of happy voices drifted over.

Raina ducked behind the maid's cart. She crouched low and peered around the cart.

Two people slipped out. Lucille leaned in to kiss the sandy-haired man, whose hands clutched her butt and pulled her closer.

Raina snickered to herself. Smoking break, huh? Was he one of the maintenance guys? The two moaned and giggled with the familiarity of old lovers. The two really should get a room. She was about to announce her presence, when the man lifted his face. She gasped. Eric Wagner! Lucille's lover was Cecelia's ex?

Her coworker had denied any knowledge of Aaron Wheeler's name. Did this mean she was in cahoots with Eric? Or was Aaron a pseudonym she didn't even know about?

All these times when Lucille had been taking a smoking break, she'd been with Eric instead. And right under Cecelia's nose too. Raina would love to be a fly on the wall when the resort owner found out about these two.

She had to get out of here before the two realized they weren't alone. The distance from the maid's cart to the entrance was one vast empty space. She was a trapped duck.

One more loud kiss, and Lucille pulled away. "We need to stop. Raina should be done with the last two suites by now."

Eric pulled Lucille closer, rubbing his groin against her hips like a cat against a pole. "Is that the cute Chinese girl with the curly hair?"

Lucille stiffened. "You met her, huh?"

Eric nuzzled Lucille's neck. "You have nothing to worry about, babe. I like a woman with some junk in her trunk. That girl is all skin and bones."

Raina ducked back behind the cart. If she watched anymore, she would have to bleach her eyes out later. A few more minutes of sighs and kisses later, Lucille sounded mollified under Eric's attention.

"Did you clean out Sui Yuk Liang's room yet?" Eric asked.

"No," Lucille said, her voice husky.

"What's still in the room?"

"Everything. Cecelia's afraid to touch anything after the police came by. Why are you asking all these questions?"

"Sui Yuk and I were drinking buddies, that's all. I have eyes for no one but you."

"Uh-huh. Then why can't we tell Cecelia about us?"

"Oh, babe, now is not the time. With the economy, I can't find a job anywhere else."

"You can always move in with me. I know how to take care of my man."

Someone should dump a bucket of ice water in the woman's panties for making all women look like suckers.

"I don't want to be a kept man," Eric said, starting to sound irritated. "The timing is just not good for me right now."

Raina risked another peek at the couple. As if any time would be good for a scrub. Eric frowned as he pulled away from the embrace. Lucille hunched her shoulders as she pleaded with puppy eyes.

Eric swaggered toward the doorway as if he already had what he came for. "I have to go."

Raina tensed, and her heartbeat jumped. *Don't turn around.*

"Wait, honey!" Lucille called out.

Eric turned, a cocky half smiled that froze when he saw Raina huddled by the maid's cart. Raina gave him a watery smile. He jerked as if she'd given him the finger.

"Honey?" Lucille said again.

"Someone has been listening to us the entire time. Take care of her or I will." Eric stalked out of the room without another word.

Raina shivered at the threat in his voice.

"Who's here?" Lucille asked sharply.

Raina stood with both hands up in the air. "Don't shoot. I was loading up on toilet paper when the two of you stumbled out the closet."

Lucille scowled and crossed the room in quick steps until she was inches from Raina's face. "If Cecelia finds out about us, you're gonna wish you'd never stepped foot on the resort."

"But I thought we were buds?" Raina asked, trying to lighten up the mood.

"Over my dead body."

AFTER EFFECTIVELY ENDING their working relationship, Lucille made no effort to hide her sloppiness. By the time three o'clock rolled around, Raina was so tense, a knife would have bounced off her shoulder blades. While Eric didn't make another appearance, she hightailed it out of the resort like a con making a break for freedom. Talk about a toxic work environment.

Raina was on her way to the Sullivans when her grandma called to say Muyang Yao made contact. She made a U-turn on Ashford Street and drove to the senior center. There was plenty of time to catch up with Brenda later.

Po Po met her in the lobby of the senior condo complex with the dowager bump, half-moon glasses, and the pimp cane. "Muyang will be here in a few minutes." She led them through the double set of doors that opened into the attached Gold Springs Senior Center.

"Where do I hide?" Raina asked, scanning the open floor plan of the recreation room.

Frank Small and his friend played chess in one corner, sliding sideways glances and hidden smiles in their direction. Another elderly man monitored the police scanner by the window, a notebook on his lap and a walkie-talkie within easy reach. You would think he was the dispatcher from his focused concentration. In front of the fireplace, Janice Tally raised an eyebrow at Po Po's entrance and went back to rolling yarn from her walker bag.

It was her grandma's turf alright, and Raina couldn't help but wonder if Po Po posted her posse in the room to trap Muyang. But unlike her grandma, a couple of her friends had the frail thin look of the elderly who didn't exercise much. Frank, the ex-military officer, was the only one who still held any physical presence, but she didn't relish the idea of explaining to her best friend, Eden, who was his granddaughter, what happened if he fell.

"Put this on." Po Po handed her a salt and pepper wig. "You can sit with your back to the room."

Raina stuffed her long curly black hair into the wig. "But I can't see anything. I'll just sit with a newspaper tn front of my face. This thing is hot." With the fireplace going and the heater turned up, it felt like a long-haired cat decided to take a nap on her head.

"Can you be more obvious? Geez, do I need to teach you how to be sneaky? Just help Janice roll yarn. Hunched over and so the wig partially covers your face."

Po Po sat in the middle of the room, playing with her smart phone to pass the time. Raina was thankful Janice didn't make any attempt at small talk. As the minutes ticked by, the recreation room became quiet as a tomb.

The outer doors swooshed open, and Raina could hear approaching footsteps. As one, all heads turned toward the double doors, and just as hastily, everyone returned to their activities as if on cue. Raina tugged more yarn from the skein and rolled it around the ball in her hand.

"Hi, Wong Po Po," Fanny called out. "Why is Raina wearing a wig?"

Raina glanced up to see the foreign exchange student gaping at her.

Po Po grabbed Fanny's forearm. "Come help me with the puzzle, granddaughter," she said. She bent close and whispered rapidly.

Fanny's eyes grew rounder, and she glanced around with unsuppressed excitement. She bobbed her head with a wide smile. Oh great. Another player invited to a game of Cops and Robbers.

A shadow flickered in her peripheral vision, and Raina ducked her head, focusing on the yarn like it was a lifeline. A bead of sweat ran down the side of her face, but she was afraid to call attention to herself by wiping it. From between the strands of the wig, she peered at the doorway and saw the woman who'd been hiding in Cecelia's closet.

Muyang clutched the thin gold chain around her neck as her eyes scanned the room. She chewed her lip as if waiting for an invitation. Her eyes were wide like a mouse watching an approaching tiger. Poor thing. Raina had no idea what she would do if she were in Muyang's shoes—desperate for information, but with no proof she wasn't walking into a trap. She had to be BL's birth mother.

Po Po waved from her seat, but Muyang jerked her head to indicate the hall behind her. Without waiting for a response, she spun on her heels and walked out of sight. Po Po shuffled after Muyang. The picture-perfect helpless little old lady.

Raina bolted after her grandma, knocking over the ball of yarn on her lap. She stopped short at the doorway, afraid to interrupt their conversation, only to have Fanny crash into her from behind. Raina tumbled onto her hands and knees with Fanny screeching behind her, making enough noise to spook a tiger. Raina looked up in time to see Muyang flipping Po Po into a fireman carry. The mousy woman morphed to a crouching tiger.

"Sorry, sorry," Fanny said, picking herself up off the floor. She hobbled and fell back onto the floor, clutching her ankle.

A flash of fear squeezed Raina's heart. She scrambled to her feet. She had to get to the grappling pair before Muyang made off with her grandma.

Po Po tossed a handful of small cylinders on the floor. She kicked and bucked. Muyang shifted her weight, struggling to keep a hold on Po Po. Her foot crunched on several of the cylinders. A white haze mushroomed around them. A shrill alarm blasted throughout the hall.

Raina jumped at the sound. Fanny must have pulled the fire alarm. She plunged into the white haze, grabbing at blurred shapes. She tugged at a fistful of cloth, not caring if it was Po Po or Muyang. The cloth ripped. *Thump.* Po Po screamed.

Footsteps clattered in the hall behind them. Po Po's friends must have scrambled out of the recreation room. A blast of cold air threw a strand of Raina's hair across her face. A large brown arm snaked out and hauled Raina off her feet.

Raina bucked. "No! Help my grandma."

Frank pulled Raina out of the haze and

plunged back in. A heartbeat later, he carried out a grinning Po Po. Her grandma looked like a doll in his arms.

Raina shivered, goose pimples forming on her forearms. She let out a rattled breath. "Are you okay?"

Po Po nodded. "Good thing I stuffed my backpack with a pillow. I could have landed on my back. I didn't realize Muyang knows kung fu." She broke into a toothy grin. "I'm not a bad ninja myself. Like my ninja fog? Dry ice encased in a water tube. Works like a charm, huh?"

"So charming"—Raina pointed at Fanny—"it overcame her sensibilities."

Po Po peered at the prone figure on the floor. "Oh, come on. It's not even my good stuff. How does she expect to be my protégé if she couldn't even handle a little horseplay?"

Frank picked up a swooning Fanny from off the floor. A wailing fire truck pulled into the parking lot as they made their way out of the senior center.

Janice glided over with the aid of her walker. "This is it, Bonnie Wong. I'm petitioning the Board to revoke your membership."

"You can't do that. Membership is part of the HOA dues for the condo," Po Po said.

"We'll see about that. Probation meant any infraction. If I had my way, you would have been thrown out after the one finger chili incident."

"It wasn't even my finger!"

"Tell that to the judge," Janice said, gliding away.

Raina took a deep, cleansing breath. She wasn't surprised at Janice's reaction to her grandma's antics. This she understood. But Muyang's flip from mouse to predator? Not only did she not see this coming, but it must mean the mom was getting desperate. And a desperate person was a dangerous person. It was time to warn the Sullivans and to have a chat with Matthew.

17

DELUSIONS

Raina pulled up next to the Sullivans' driveway. The Christmas lights were off and the inflatable snowman and reindeers slumped against each other in an unruly pile on the front lawn. The curtains were drawn, with only a small light spilling out into the night from the rear. Raina chewed her lip, debating whether or not she should knock.

While she and Brenda were good friends, it still seemed intrusive to ask for details to their current problem with the law. They hadn't asked for her help, but they were going to get it regardless. And she couldn't very well help without the details.

Tap! Tap!

Raina jumped at the sound coming from the driver side window. She was so busy watching the house, she hadn't notice anyone coming up to her car.

With the streetlight behind the person, she couldn't make out the face. The person made a hand-cranking motion. Right, like she was going to open the car door to a stranger on a deserted street. This was when the too-stupid-to-live girl always got killed in a slasher movie.

"It's Toni Moody. We should talk." She took a couple steps back as if finally aware her face was hidden in the shadow.

"Okay," Raina yelled, hoping the private investigator would be able to hear her. "There's a Peet's outside of the subdivision on the right. Follow me." Raina started the car. While Toni hadn't appeared threatening in their first meeting several days ago, it was better to chat when there were other people around. She waited until Toni turned on her headlights and pulled out onto the road.

During the short drive to the coffee house, Raina mentally reviewed their first encounter. Toni had asked questions about Cecelia's business practices. At first, Raina thought a government agency hired Toni to help with their investigation. Now she wasn't so sure.

They ordered their drinks—more iced coffee for Raina and chamomile tea for Toni. There were only two other patrons at the place and they were plugged into their laptops with headsets. The barista was busy restacking the shelves. The overhead pendant lights spotlighted their small table so the rest of the coffeehouse seemed to fade into the background.

"How's your coffee?" Toni asked.

"Good," Raina said. "What were you doing outside the Sullivans' home? Or do you think they worked for Cecelia too?"

Toni raised an eyebrow. "Are you always this sarcastic? Or do you just miss me?"

Raina shrugged. She was tired and out of sorts. Tomorrow was Christmas, and she hadn't even had time to prepare for it yet. Besides, it wasn't like she owed the private investigator anything. However, she would like to know what exactly Toni was investigating. "It has been an eventful day."

"I would say that's an understatement. It's not every day the senior center gets filled with the off gassing from dry ice and water." Toni sipped her tea casually.

"It was you—you were spying on me at the resort earlier. Why are you following me?"

"You have good instincts. Most people would just shake it off, thinking it was their imagination. Ever considered working as a private investigator?"

Raina ignored Toni's attempt to introduce another topic. "Are you really investigating the resort or are you after something else?"

"Let me put my cards on the table. I'm

hired to find evidence against Cecelia to close down her resort. I believe she has another set of books. If the feds were able to put Al Capone in jail for tax evasion, then there's already a cell with Cecelia's name on it."

"But what does this have to do with me?"

"You seem to be on the fringes of my investigation. Every time I turn around, you are talking to someone I'm interested in or sneaking into places I want to be at. What exactly are you doing, Miss Sun? Are you friend or foe?"

Raina took a long sip of coffee, dragging it out to give herself time to think. If Toni was telling the truth, and Raina had no reason to believe otherwise, then they held some common interests. But this didn't make them allies. "I could ask you the same thing."

Toni gave her a crooked smile. "Trust requires you to give more than you get in return."

Raina snorted. "What are you going to give me?"

"The truth. I believe Cecelia was involved in a child kidnapping case."

Heat rose from Raina's chest to her face. Her client must be Muyang Yao. It was the only explanation. "Did you help Muyang Yao get away? She tried to kidnap my grandmother."

"I knew you would catch on. Like I said, you're sharp. For what it's worth, I don't think she meant to hurt your grandma. I have no leads on who might have her baby, or even if there is a baby. Cecelia is not talking. Neither is her ex or the head housekeeper. When Muyang saw the ad, it was like a curtain fell over her. She became Mr. Hyde in a sense. She was sure the baby had to be hers."

Raina took a deep breath. Anger wouldn't help the situation even if she felt like giving Muyang a whack on the backside. "The ad was for information on the baby's mother, Sui Yuk Liang. Why would Muyang think the baby is hers?"

"Sui Yuk and Muyang were friends. Mostly

they stuck together because there was no one else. Muyang knew Sui Yuk had a difficult pregnancy, so she wasn't surprised Sui Yuk had a stillbirth. However, she never visited her friend at the hospital. Something about bad juju. So I can't verify whether or not Sui Yuk actually had a live birth."

"And then later Muyang had a stillbirth too. Not exactly good stats for a resort claiming to be 'the premier women wellness and birth center for Gold Country USA.' How did Muyang react to her own stillbirth?"

"This is where things get tricky. Muyang was told she had a stillbirth. Her memory was spotty because of all the drugs. A month post-partum, Cecelia asked her to leave."

"Where's the baby? It's not like the doctor could get rid of the remains without her permission." Or maybe they did. If Cecelia had something on the medical staff she'd imported from the Philippines, they might do as she directed.

"She remembers holding the body before

they took it away. She lost a couple days because they continued to drug her afterward, claiming she was a threat to herself."

Raina frowned. She was under the assumption Cecelia helped Sui Yuk swap the babies. But what if she were wrong? "Do you believe Muyang had a live birth? Could this all be in her head?"

"I believed her at first, but now I'm not sure. I was hired to find wrongdoings at the resort and turn it over to authorities. I could fulfill my obligation to my client without getting involved in this aspect of the investigation."

"It's been a couple months since everything went down at the resort. Why now? Why didn't Muyang do something earlier?"

"I think she was still coming to terms with losing the baby. But when Muyang saw Sui Yuk with a newborn at Bullseye, the flood gates opened."

Raina jerked, knocking over the plastic

cup. Ice and coffee spilled across the table, ran down one side, and soaked her jeans and underwear. She jumped up, swiping at her crotch with a damp napkin. Real smooth, Sherlock.

The barista came over with a towel to clean up the mess. Raina apologized, and they moved to another table. She shifted on her chair, her wet underwear chafing against her skin. Muyang could have seen Sui Yuk on another day. It didn't have to be the Saturday she died. "When was she at Bullseye?"

"A couple weeks ago. Muyang initially only wanted to talk to Sui Yuk but grew suspicious when her former buddy avoided her like the plague. According to her, Sui Yuk Liang shouldn't have had a baby."

"But this doesn't mean anything sinister. Chinese culture is very superstitious. With Muyang's stillbirth, no new mom would want their baby around her."

Toni shrugged, to show that she wasn't judging. "A simple DNA test would lay the maternity question to rest. Do you know where Sui Yuk Liang's baby is?"

Raina raised an eyebrow. Real smooth. If her client didn't try to kidnap Po Po, she might have fallen for the buddy-buddy act. If Toni didn't already guess BL was with the Sullivans, she wasn't going to enlighten her. "Where is Muyang now?"

"I don't know. She was staying at the Sandman Motel by the train tracks, but she hasn't been back there in a couple of days."

"Do you think your client might be delusional?"

Toni's lips pressed into a grim line. She didn't answer, but her silence was louder than anything she could have said.

Muyang must have sent Sui Yuk the threatening note. And now she had gone rogue and believed Po Po to have information on her baby. Raina shivered. Who knew how much damage an unstable postpartum woman could do to a seventy-five-year-old grandma.

THE NEXT MORNING, Raina shifted on the unforgiving antique chair in the lobby of the senior condo complex. She came over early as planned for the carpool to San Francisco for the Wong's Christmas dinner. By the time she got home last night, she only had time to send a quick text to the Sullivans and her grandma, pleading with them to be careful of strangers.

She peered through the glass doors, but didn't see Matthew's Jeep. He must be running late. Again. No matter how punctual he might be when it came to his job, his watch ran on a drained battery when it came to his personal life. It was a trait that drove her bonkers. Asking to meet fifteen minutes earlier only meant she would have to wait an extra fifteen minutes on top of his usual tardiness.

Fanny read the flyers on the bulletin boards while Po Po and Maggie Louie spoke with another resident about the upcoming New Year's Eve party at the senior center. All four didn't seem to notice the gazillion flashing colored lights scattered throughout the place that could give a less hearty soul a seizure.

The decorating committee must have had a decorations fight and flung whatever they could on the walls. The pink metallic tree competed with the six-foot Charlie Brown Christmas tree for the place of honor, while several ugly Christmas sweaters were pinned on a line running across the wall behind the check-in desk. Someone had even replaced the white doilies with green and red checkered ones.

A Jeep pulled up next to the curb. Raina hopped to her feet. "Matthew is here," she called out, interrupting the quiet buzz of conversation. It was rude, but her skin felt tight like she had been waiting for her turn at the chopping block. It was time to hit the road.

As she reached for the lobby door, Matthew appeared on the other side. For a split second their eyes met through the glass pane. Time froze as she stood like a mannequin with an outstretched arm. The strand of colored lights around the doorframe added to the storefront effect. The picture-perfect boyfriend.

Raina blinked and the moment disappeared. Her smile wobbled, as if she wanted to cry. Her reaction should be ridiculous, except it felt so right.

Matthew opened the door and a whiff of coffee drifted over. Yum. Hazelnut. "Three creams and two sugars."

Now there was a full-grown frog in her throat. She averted her eyes and mumbled thanks.

The grandmas made their good-byes and headed toward them, still chatting as if they hadn't seen each other in years.

"Po Po, where is Fanny?" Raina asked.

"She was here just a minute ago. I'll text her to come outside," Po Po said.

Raina swept her gaze around the lobby one last time. No Fanny. She caught up with the rest of the group. As she reached for the handle of the front passenger door, the window rolled down. She started in surprise.

Fanny's bright smile appeared from within. "Do you need something?"

"Uh, no," Raina mumbled and stepped back to climb into the backseat after her grandma. She pressed her lips together to stop the frown from forming.

She nursed the coffee, letting the warmth seep into her hands but not to her heart. Sometimes Matthew could be rather sweet, but how much of the sweetness was an act? It didn't feel natural to question his motives.

Fanny's giggles were matched by the grandmas' hushed whispers. Matthew stared at the road, responding to Fanny in monosyllables when pressed to do so. She carried on the entire conversation by herself.

Raina closed her eyes and leaned against the window, willing herself to sleep. She'd spent the night wrangling with the sheets. Her nightmares alternating between Muyang running off with her grandma and Matthew throwing BL like a football to China.

She was walking that fine line again where one side held safety and the other vibrated with danger. And like before, she could feel the desire to play peek-a-boo with danger just for those rare moments when the air pulsated with energy. Of being alive. Of being young and whole. Her grandma probably courted danger for the exact same reasons.

If she told her grandma about Muyang's instability, Po Po would want to use herself as bait. If she didn't tell Po Po, and something happened to her, Raina would never forgive herself. Why did protecting Po Po always come down to keeping secrets from her?

NEW RAIN

The red Chinese lanterns on her Uncle Sain's restaurant glowed like a beacon in the mostly deserted streets in Chinatown. The rolling gray fog dampened the aromatic spices, rotting vegetables, and a hint of sewage that seemed to cling to this part of the city.

Uncle Sain and his family stood by the door, greeting the rest of the extended family. Uncle Sain preferred his Chinese name to his American name. It probably had to do with the fact that he lived and worked in Chinatown where things like family names and old customs still mattered. His kids, on the other hand, seemed to work harder than the rest of the cousins to prove they were more American than anyone else.

"Raina, so you finally show your face around here," Uncle Sain said.

"She's busy spending her millions, Dad. You know how it is. They forget about the little people like us," Cousin Jung-yee said.

Moisture clung in wet droplets in Raina's curly hair, but her mouth was dry. She'd thought the attacks would come later in the evening after her nerves became taut from the wait. Her fingers clutched the wrapped Jiggle Me Doll in front of her like a broken shield.

"You're anything but little, Sain," Po Po said, poking his rotund stomach. "Jung-yee, you really need to stop sucking lemons. It makes you look like the bitter stepsister in Cinderella. Don't worry, when I die, I'll leave my millions to you."

Jung-yee's face lit up. "Really, Grandma?"

"Sure, but you'll need to be at my beck and call twenty-four-seven for two years first. Like how Rainy cared for Ah Gong."

"Mah Mah," Jung-yee whined, as if using her paternal grandma's title would soften her up. "It's just so unfair. Why do I have to work at this dump while she got to quit her job?" She didn't seem to notice her father's frown at her reference to the family restaurant. "I'm sick of smelling like fried rice."

"Life's not fair and things are not always what they seem, sweetie. Maybe you should go back to school," Po Po said, hooking an arm through Raina's and towing them into the restaurant. She leaned over to whisper, "She must have gotten her tongue from her mom."

"How did you get her to drop the lawsuit?" Raina whispered back as her eyes scanned the room.

"By threatening to give my millions to you too," Po Po said with a hint of laughter in her voice. "Word got out to the other grandchildren fast enough."

Raina sneaked a sideways glance at her grandma. "And would it be okay if word got out about Ah Gong's other family?"

Po Po stiffened, interrupting their steady progress across the room. Matthew and his grandma bumped against them from behind at the sudden stop. There was a moment of apologies and embarrassed smiles.

By the time everyone had straightened themselves out, there was no more time for further discussion with her grandma. In other words, Raina's role was still confined to the greedy grandchild who finagled her grandfather into leaving out her cousins in his will.

Her mom and sisters chatted easily among the family members. Her brother was MIA, which meant he was with his girlfriend's family. Lila, her niece and the baby of the family, circulated from one set of arms to another, clutching her new Jiggle Me doll. When an aunt wanted to take the toy for a test drive, Lila held the doll behind her back and shouted, "Mine!" in a clear voice that cut through all the conversation in the room.

Raina smiled. What she wouldn't give to have the concerns of a toddler. After a few more minutes of small talk where everyone tiptoed around her, she got a scotch on the rocks and found an empty table in the back. Dinner wouldn't start for another thirty minutes, and she was running out of steam.

Matthew circulated among her family with more ease than she did. He'd grown up with many of them, a de facto cousin himself. Fanny trailed after him until Tobias, one of her cousins, gestured for her to join their group drinking in the back corner and playing blackjack. The woman was too cute to be a wallflower.

The clicking of mahjong tiles on Raina's right caught her attention, and she turned to see her grandma in a rousing game with an aunt, a great uncle, and Maggie Louie. It seemed as if everyone was enjoying themselves, except for her. She was just thankful there was no open hostility. Once the food came out, she could pretend to be obsessed with stuffing her face to prevent anyone from snubbing her.

Her gaze returned to a laughing Matthew at the bar. His smile was carefree with a readied lightness as if he was with people he'd always trusted. Like his family. Aside from Maggie, Matthew didn't have anyone else or any place to call home. But here, he was with people who had known him as a baby and shaped him as an adult. Though he'd been busy saving the world when he worked for the feds, he was still on the invite list for birthdays, holiday dinners, and weddings.

Her trembling hand clinked the ice against the glass when she brought the scotch to her lips. Even though he clearly loved her, his father wasn't the only reason why Matthew rejected her. No, he rejected her and chose her family instead. An ugly breakup between them would mean the Wongs might reject him, and Matthew would never let that happen.

As she watched Matthew, his earlier words about growing up in a family not his own took on new meaning. Did BL belong to Sui Yuk Liang or to Muyang Yao? And there was money involved if what Eric Wagner said after Po Po beat him up was true. Someone was willing to pay to get their hands on BL, but did this person want the infant alive or dead?

Money had a way of turning even the mildest of Sunday school teachers into foaming wild animals under the right circumstances. Look at her family and how they circled around Ah Gong in his deathbed.

The hairs on the back of Raina's neck stiffened as if she were tiptoeing across a grave. This was not the place or time to have these kind of thoughts. The Cantonese Christmas music piping through the mounted speakers did little to chase her dark thoughts away. She gazed around the length of the restaurant, looking for a distraction.

Someone tugged at her sweater. "New Rain! New Rain!"

Raina's smile could light up the room. There was only one person who thought the literal translation of her Chinese name was her English name. "Hi sweetie." She grabbed her niece, Lila, and swung the child onto her lap. "Hey, what happened to your chin?" She tickled the toddler's neck.

Lila giggled and reached out to wiggle her stubby little fingers under her aunt's chin.

Raina widened her eyes and clasped a hand on her chin. "Oh no! My chin is gone, too."

Lila stuffed the foot of her Jiggle Me Doll into her mouth to hide her chortle.

Raina hugged the child, placing a kiss on the top of her head.

The child's entire body vibrated with laughter.

"Lila, come here to Mommy," Cassie called out, breaking into the horseplay.

Raina glanced up to find her sister, mom,

and Jung-yee studying them with matching expressions of disapproval.

"Come here, sweetie," Cassie said. "We don't want to bother your auntie."

"I can watch her for a few minutes," Raina said.

Lila bounced on her lap. "Again, New Rain. Again. Find chin."

Cassie held out her hands. "Come."

Lila shifted her eyes between her mom and her aunt, finally aware of the tension. She sucked her thumb and clung to her doll.

Cassie hauled her daughter off of her aunt's lap. "Daddy is looking for you, sweetie." She marched off without another word.

Jung-yee smirked.

"You need to ask your sister before making off with Lila. Since you're not a mom, I know you don't understand how frightening it could be for your child to disappear without any warning," Mom said, her voice dripping with irritation.

Raina licked her lips. This had nothing to

do with Lila. "Look, there is more going on here than you know. I have nothing to do with Ah Gong leaving me the bulk of his money. I haven't even touched a cent of it. He left it to me for a very specific purpose."

"What purpose?" Mom asked. "If it concerns the family, Rainy, you should tell us."

"She's lying," Jung-yee said. "If there's really this big family secret she keeps hinting at, then how come Grandma isn't talking about it? Mah Mah isn't the type to hide things. Just admit it, Raina, you manipulated a dying old man."

Raina searched the room for a pair of friendly eyes. Several relatives actually stopped talking to stare back at her, with curious expressions, but no one came over to rescue her from this interrogation. Po Po gave her a sideways glance, but quickly averted her eyes when she realized Raina was watching her.

Her eyes narrowed. What right did her cousin and her mom have to interrogate her like this? To publicly embarrass her for doing what was asked of her? The selfish person in this situation was Ah Gong for his self-indulgence, and now her grandma for wanting to pretend they had an exemplary marriage. What right did her grandparents have to put her in this kind of position?

"Right, and you were just so selfless when you only managed to visit Ah Gong two times the last two months he was alive," Raina said to her cousin. "Gee, I can see why he only left you one dollar."

Jung-yee flushed a deep red. For a second, it seemed as if her eyes were about to pop off their sockets. "You're such a bit—"

"Raina!" Mom snapped. "There's no need to aggravate your cousin."

Jung-yee crossed her arms, huffing in a way to imply she was mortally wronged. It would have been funny, except her mom was also glaring at her.

"Oh really?" Raina asked. She couldn't seem to keep the bite from her voice. "Do you think it's okay for someone to inherit"—she made air quotes with her fingers—"a boatload of money because she's a relative? By your definition, your stepdaughter should be in your will. Cassie only visited Ah Gong once the entire time he was at the hospital. Once, Mom, just once."

Mom clenched her jaw. "The business with your half-sister is not open for discussion. It's been ten years since I last laid eyes on her. She's not part of our lives anymore."

How exactly could Raina forget the older sister who helped wipe her nose or gave her the hugs and kisses her mom had withheld from her during her childhood?

"Oh my god, you kept one of your stupid spreadsheets again." Jung-yee mocked, breaking off Raina's train of thought. "Don't you have anything better to do with your time?"

Raina gave her an ugly smirk, glad for an excuse to pack her half-sister to the compartment of things she ignored. "I say my time was put to good use. After all, I have the boatload, and you don't even have a bucket."

Jung-yee sputtered, spun on her heels, and marched off. Mom shook her head as if she was disappointed in Raina again and followed her cousin.

Raina blinked at the burning in the back of her eyes. Deep breaths. In. Out. She swallowed, trying to clear the lump in her throat. In. Out. The conversation around her continued to buzz, but everyone avoided eye contact. In. Out—

She couldn't breathe. Her blood roared in her ears. She had to get out of here. Both hands reached for the temples on her head.

Thunk!

Her gaze followed the glass tumbler bouncing on the carpet, spilling ice cubes and alcohol across her gray leather boots. Her hand must have knocked it off the table, but there was no memory of the glass against her skin.

She stood, fully intending to clean up the

mess, but before she realized it, she was running. Through the narrow hall, to the kitchen, and out the backdoor.

Once outside, she slowed. The thick fog blanketed the entire alley in a pale imitation of a dreamy landscape. She stumbled for another five feet until the white plastic patio set popped out from the fog. She collapsed into the chair, grateful she knew her way around her uncle's restaurant. The two summers of waiting tables in high school weren't entirely a waste after all.

Raina didn't know what came over her. After being silent for so long, she wanted to jump off the ledge just to get it over with. It didn't help the situation that her grandma wanted to cover up her late husband's shame. Argh! She could spit—

The backdoor squealed like fingers scratching on a chalkboard. The noise echoed in the alley, seeming to come from the fog itself. She wrapped her arms around herself. Her cashmere sweater and corduroy pants were no match for the damp and cold that rolled in from the ocean.

Footsteps headed away from her. Her shoulders sagged. Probably one of the workers taking out the trash or on a smoking break.

Raina knew she should apologize to her mother. If nothing else, it would at least keep the peace in the Sun household. But a part of her rebelled against the unfairness of the situation. She was tired of being the good girl. The one who followed her elders' instructions without questioning it. Geez, she was starting to sound like Jung-yee with her whining.

"Are you okay?" someone said in front of her.

Raina jerked, almost tipping the flimsy chair backwards. A shadow stepped out from the fog and reached a hand to steady her. Her heart took a flying leap. She froze as the thought hit her that she was in a dimly lit alley with a stranger. Even if her screams were heard, the fog would hide her from view.

19

CHRISTMAS BLUES

The stranger stepped back as if sensing her unease. His face was half in the shadows, but what she could see was open and friendly. Tall, dark, and handsome. Even the way he walked out of the fog had a fairytale quality to it.

She gave herself a mental headshake. Prince Charming didn't exist. "Yes, I'm fine. Don't worry about me. Just carry on." She waved her hand to dismiss him. Maybe it was a little rude, but how was she to know he wasn't a serial killer?

The stranger pulled out a chair and sat. "My name is Blue. We spoke before, on the phone. Your uncle—"

"You're the one who called me a hooker."

He tugged at the collar of his sweater. "Sorry about that. Your Uncle Anthony said that you were single. And since I'm single—"

"And so we have that much in common, huh?" Raina raised an eyebrow. She sounded like a grump, but she didn't care. A blind date was the last thing she needed.

"It's that bad, huh? Families can do that to you sometimes."

Raina's face burned. Did everyone know she was the black sheep of the family? She glanced up into a pair of warm gold-flecked hazel eyes framed in black lashes. The stranger smiled, flashing a deep dimple on his right cheek. A lock of black hair curled on his temple. He had those distinct features of mixed children. She liked to call it Caucasian with a twist.

Perhaps it was the understanding look in

his eyes, or her desire to unburden herself, but without even being aware she'd made a decision, Raina told Blue everything. She unloaded the entire sob story about Ah Gong's will and what he wanted her to do with the money.

Blue's eyes blinked several times when she got to the part about Ah Gong's secret wife, son, and grandchild in China, but he didn't interrupt her. Gosh, this man could be a keeper.

"To top it off, Po Po didn't even come over to defend me." Her voice wobbled, but she held it together. It was one thing to confess her shameful family secret to a stranger, but another thing to do it while weeping like a ninny. "If she'd explained the whole convoluted arrangement, my mom and my sister could stop hounding me to share"—she made air quotes with her hands—"my largess."

"Maybe your grandma didn't say anything because she felt betrayed. It took you almost two years to get around to telling her." Blue shrugged out of his black wool jacket and draped it over Raina's shoulders. "Sometimes family can be your worst enemy."

Raina tucked her chilled hands into the pockets. The jacket still held his body heat, and the warmth seeped through her sweater. Was his last comment referring to her? Was Po Po secretly angry with her? "Aren't you cold?"

"You have been out here longer than me. It'd take a few more minutes yet before I feel the cold."

He was probably lying through his pearly whites, but Raina was more than happy to snuggle in the jacket. "I didn't exactly lie. I just didn't tell her the truth."

He raised an eyebrow. "How would you feel if she did the same to you?"

Raina squirmed under his gaze. Po Po couldn't have handled the truth. She'd needed time to process her husband's death at the time. "Do you think I did the right thing?"

"It was right at the time for you. That's all that matters."

Raina sighed. "Thank you."

"Have you thought about meeting this other family? For all you know, they might feel the same way about your family."

"What do you mean?"

"What if your granddad fooled his other wife too? What if the other wife thinks she's the number one wife, and your grandma was the interloper?"

Raina's mouth fell open. The idea was so crazy, it had merit. She snapped it shut at Blue's pitying look. "Po Po and Ah Gong were married."

"I thought polygamy was common in China."

"No, it's not. Sometimes rich men would set up a separate household for their mistresses, but these women are never wives."

"I don't understand. What difference does it make if the mistress is a wife or not?"

"It does—both legally and socially.

Women might tolerate a mistress in their social circle if the man is rich or powerful enough, but their sympathies always lie with the wife."

He was silent for a moment as if considering her words. "Cheating is cheating no matter how you spin it, right? I'm sorry you were caught up in the drama."

She gave him a thin smile. "In dark corners we find ourselves, and more knowledge lights our way."

"Gotta love a woman who can quote Yoda. You're a keeper. Just remember that a truth depends on your point of view."

Raina snorted in an unladylike manner. Was he flirting with her? Why? Her other female cousins were much more attractive with their hourglass figures and straight hair. Raina's boyish frame and curly bush of hair made her looked more like a walking lollipop than a dainty Chinese doll. "So what's your story? Are you related to one of my cousins?"

"No relation to your family, thank God,"

he said. At her raised eyebrow, he amended, "It'd be weird to show interest in a family member even if it is a cousin of a cousin."

Raina blushed. He was flirting with her.

"I'm Anthony Wong's contractor for the bump out of his office space," Blue continued. "The people next door moved out, and he decided to use the entire second floor of the building for his law firm."

"Where's your family?" Raina asked. "Why aren't you spending Christmas with them?"

"Mom is a wannabe actress living in a trailer in Tracy and dad is gone with the wind. I'm as footloose and fancy free as an orphan."

"Oh, I'm sorry. I don't mean to bring up... I thought you would tell me your family is from overseas."

He grinned at her, exposing a crooked top tooth. "Don't worry about it. I did spend my childhood in Italy where my mom was trying to get into opera singing. The woman could barely sing the ABC song without cracking a windshield. My childhood is done and over with. I survived it. The relationship with my mom only includes the few times a year I send her money. There are no calls and no interactions. It suits both of us."

Raina couldn't imagine never speaking with her mom again. In some ways Blue's relationship with his mom was worse than death. At least Raina could visit her dad's grave and burn incense to feed his spirit and ask for his protection. She'd never felt alone because her ancestors walked with her. To willingly cut off his family wasn't something she understood.

"What's your last name?"

"Pufferneck," he said. "Blue Pufferneck."

Raina's mouth dropped. Did his parents hate him? A bubble of mirth escaped her lips and before she could stop herself, she laughed until her shoulders shook. She tried stopping herself by turning away from his twinkling eyes, but to no avail. She clutched her thighs, digging her nails into her leg. The pain finally calmed her down. It felt good to release the tension.

"I'm so sorry. I don't know what came over me. For someone so attractive, I was expecting something... sexier."

He held out his hand. "Sebastian de Amor"

She shook it. "Really?"

"It's Sebastian Luc, but please call me Superfly."

Raina rolled her eyes. "I'm not calling you Superfly. I feel silly even saying it out loud."

"What's wrong with silly? Call me anything but the crab in *Little Mermaid*. It was the play my mom was in when she was pregnant with me. Just call me Blue. You smile when you say it."

Did she? Raina hadn't even noticed it. What she noticed was that he still held her hand. More like enclosed it with a warmth and gentleness that was a surprising contrast to his comedic performance. And his voice was smooth with a trace of a European accent. She could listen to his voice all day.

The door behind them banged open.

Matthew called out, "Rainy, the banquet is starting. They were just done with the cold dish when I left to look for you. If we hurry, we might get back before the deep-fried crab balls. When it's family style, the good dishes disappear fast."

Raina extracted her hand, blushing with guilt. She averted her face from Matthew's penetrating look when she strolled past him.

The rest of the evening passed in a haze of good food and cold wine. She kept an eye on Po Po, but she didn't seem to be nursing any secret grudge. By the time she got home, she dismissed Blue's comment. How could a stranger know her family as well as she did?

THE NEXT MORNING Raina was once again preparing the maid's cart by herself at the resort. Lucille had texted that she was running late. Right. She was probably somewhere getting her freak on with Eric.

Raina sighed as she stacked the rolls of toilet paper. Why was she having all these uncharitable thoughts lately? Especially at the happiest time of the year. At least the Christmas dinner was done and over with, and she would have a couple months of reprieve until the Chinese New Year banquet. Holidays were meant for selling Hallmark cards as far as she was concerned, not for actual face-to-face conversations.

And to top things off, she hadn't done laundry all week, so she had to wear the same pair of jeans she had on the day her grandma set the stink bomb off in her apartment. She was tempted to strip down to her underwear and toss them into the commercial washer in front of her. All things in life were relative. At least her underwear was clean.

Cecelia came in with Lucille close on her heels. The resort owner looked upset, but Lucille had a smug smile as if someone just gave her a foot rub.

Raina tensed, not trusting the look on her

coworker's face. Her pulse kicked up a notch as if preparing for battle.

"Come with me. I want you to take a look at something," Cecelia said.

"Um, okay," Raina said.

The resort owner spun on her heels and marched out. Raina followed Cecelia with Lucille bringing up the rear. Hadn't Lucille heard of personal space? The whiff of cigarette smoke and the breaths on her neck intensified the closer they got to Suite Eighteen.

Cecelia opened Sui Yuk Liang's room and gestured for Raina to step inside.

Raina scanned the room. Her spider sense tingled. Everything looked as it did when she was in the suite a few days earlier, except someone had taken out the trash and the police probably removed the laptop. She turned to find both Cecelia and Lucille studying her. She gave them a raised eyebrow.

"Someone stole Sui Yuk's jewelry," Cecelia said.

Raina's gaze swept the room again, but the

windows appeared locked. "Was there a break-in?"

"There was no sign of a break-in. The thief had a key," Cecelia continued.

Raina slid a glance at Lucille. Could the thief be Eric Wagner? He might not have a room key, but he had access to a key via Lucille. Or maybe the head housekeeper had been in cahoots with Eric the entire time.

Cecelia flushed and averted her gaze. "Someone told me that you showed an excessive amount of interest in the valuables in this room."

"The person misunderstood the situation," Raina said.

"I saw you taking pictures of the jewelry and computer," Lucille said. "They are probably still on her phone."

Raina gasped as understanding finally hit her. Lucille was trying to get rid of her like Eric had told her to do. "You were the one who got all excited over Sui Yuk's laptop because you wanted it for your son's

Christmas present. You have a room key too."

Cecelia studied Lucille with a furrowed brow as if suspecting her for the first time.

"The laptop is set up for Chinese. What use would I have for such a laptop?" Lucille smirked as if she'd won her case.

"You just go to the System Preferences and reset it for English. It's not rocket science to change the settings," Raina said. "I have no interest in the laptop or her jewelry."

"Tell that to the judge. If you weren't desperate for money, why would you be at a labor-intensive minimum wage job during your winter break? Especially with your fancy education."

If Lucille knew of the money Raina had inherited from Ah Gong, desperate wouldn't be the correct word to describe her. And what was wrong with working a minimum wage job for a couple weeks? It was either that or stay cooped up in her apartment with her best friend out of town and no boyfriend in sight.

"Not that it's any of your business, but I don't want to touch my savings to pay off a rather large car repair bill," Raina said. "This doesn't make me a thief."

Lucille turned to Cecelia. "We never had a theft before she started working here. All we got to do is check her phone."

Cecelia looked uncertain but finally nodded. "I'm sorry, Raina, but Lucille is right. We never had a theft before. I think it's better if you just leave."

"Wait. Are you firing me?" Raina asked. "You have no evidence other than Lucille's word that I'm interested in this laptop."

"Why don't you start on your duties?" Cecelia asked Lucille, but the tone was more of a command.

Lucille huffed in disappointment as if she'd expected to be the one to tell Raina to pack up. The door slammed shut, but there was no wind.

"There's no proof that I stole anything," Raina said.

"I'm sorry," Cecelia said. "You're a temp, but Lucille has been with me since I first opened the resort. She's a great help to me. It's much easier to replace you than her."

Raina swallowed her protest. There was no point in arguing her case when the resort owner had already made up her mind. "But what about Sonia? She has nothing to do with this. Would she be able to keep her job when she gets back?"

"I'll talk to Sonia when she gets back. Lucille said her cousin could help out for the rest of the winter break."

"Isn't it mighty convenient that Lucille's cousin is ready to swoop in after you fire me?"

"I'm not firing you. We're just parting ways."

Raina had enough of the word wrangling. "Fine. When do I collect my paycheck?"

Cecelia pulled a thick envelope out of her back pocket. "Here. I even added four hours for today. Merry Christmas."

Raina reached for the envelope and

frowned at the weight. "Please don't tell me you wrote a check for each day I was here."

"It's cash. Let's just say you never worked here by my books."

So Toni Moody was right. Cecelia probably had another set of books for her business transactions that the IRS would be more than happy to get their hands on. "Why cash?"

"Why not? You only worked here a few days. Less paperwork for me to take care of during tax season."

"Do you have the same cavalier attitude with our guests? I heard rumors that some of our guests literally show up with a suitcase of cash because the banking system in their country is not as sophisticated as ours." She made up the last comment, but the resort owner didn't have to know this.

Cecelia cocked her head as if seeing Raina clearly for the first time. "Are you trying to blackmail me?"

Raina shook her head. "I'm not a blackmailer. But if I'm able to figure this out after working here for a week, it makes me wonder who else knows about this and what they would do with the information."

"Well, I'll keep this in mind for the future. Good-bye, Raina."

"Will there be a future? You can't expect to throw cash around like a money laundering front when you're operating a legitimate business."

"Do you see me asking you for financial advice?"

"But you're stripping down to your panties to save a couple of bucks."

"A couple of bucks? Do you even know how much in taxes a business has to pay?"

"You always have to pay the piper. One way or the other."

Cecelia took a step closer. "What are you trying to say?"

Raina swallowed as she looked up at the tense expression on the resort owner's face. Maybe she should stop baiting the bear, especially since this particular bear could pound her into a hamburger. "Merry Christmas."

She left the suite with as much dignity as she could, even though she felt like a wimp for not defending herself against Lucille's accusation. She wanted to make a comment about the baby swap, but there was no proof and it was smarter to not alert Cecelia. Just as it was smarter to keep silent about Lucille and Eric...for now.

Once outside and out of view, she hunched her shoulders against the wind and jogged to her car. It wasn't like she got fired from a dream job, but it rankled her all the same that whoever wanted her away from the resort would be able to get away with this.

She started the engine and pulled out her cell phone to text her grandma while the car was warming up. "Fired from resort."

"Let me buy you breakfast," Po Po texted back.

Raina smiled at the thought of picking her grandma's brain on how to plot her revenge on Lucille and Eric. Normally she wasn't a vengeful person, but this wasn't a normal situation. A baby's future was at stake, and Cecelia wasn't the only one with something to protect.

20

A SIMPLE MAN

Raina parked across the street from the Sullivans' home. Po Po chewed on her croissant thoughtfully as she leaned over to stare out the driver's side window.

"What do you think is going on?" Po Po asked.

The neighborhood was quiet as if hung-over from too much Christmas joy. Without the cloak of darkness, the decorations on the Sullivans' house looked as if a three-year-old had vomited all over their yard. It didn't help matters to have a police cruiser parked up front.

Officer Hopper and Matthew came out with grim faces. Joe and Brenda followed behind them, their heads tilted together in a low conversation.

Raina turned off the engine. "I think they're arresting Joe."

They jogged up to the front yard. Po Po engaged Officer Hopper in a conversation so Raina could have a moment with Matthew.

Joe stepped close to his wife so their foreheads touched. He talked while tears leaked out of Brenda's eyes. Raina averted her gaze, uncomfortable at the scene before her. It wasn't like the movies. The raw fear on Brenda's face touched a part of Raina that made her thankful she wasn't in her friend's shoes.

"Come on, Matthew," Raina whispered into his ear. "We both know that Joe has nothing to do with Sui Yuk Liang's death."

"Stay out of this," Matthew whispered back, grabbing her arm and moving them away from Po Po and Officer Hopper. "There's nothing you can do here to help her."

"But—"

"The only way to help her is to find the real killer. With Brenda behind bars, the killer might think he got away with murder."

Raina's mouth fell to the floor. Her? Brenda? "What game are you playing?"

"Cops and robbers. Now let me do my job," Matthew said, brushing past her.

Joe hugged his wife good-bye, and Brenda followed Officer Hopper into her vehicle. Matthew gave Raina a significant cop look and got in the passenger side. As if the look could terrify her into hiding in a corner until the dust settled.

Joe watched the vehicle drive down the street until it disappeared from view. He shook himself as if waking from a dream and looked around like a lost little boy.

"Where is Johnny?" Raina asked. "Do we need to look for a lawyer?"

Joe swiped a finger under an eye, wiping a

tear. "They're charging Brenda with vehicular manslaughter. Oh my God. This is a nightmare." He buried his face in his hands.

"Who is watching the baby?" Po Po asked.

Joe lifted his head. "CPS took him yesterday. In the middle of opening presents. I need to go. I've got to get a lawyer."

"What can we do to help?" Raina asked.

"Pray for us," Joe said and stumbled back into his empty home.

Raina trotted back to her car. Time to put the squeeze on someone else for a change. She was getting tired of dancing to someone's puppet strings.

Po Po jogged to keep up with her. "Where are we going?"

"To Eric Wagner's trailer. I want to see if he's hiding the jewelry there."

AFTER RAINA PARKED in a guest spot, she called the resort to ask for Eric Wagner. The front desk person said Eric was working on the south end of the property. She rattled off a fake phone number to the front desk person and asked Eric to call her back.

She crouched lower behind the shadow of the native oak. It started to drizzle, and the ground, already moist from last night's rain, seemed to grow wetter by the minute. A light fog drifted around them, giving the trees a romantic look. It was the perfect weather for a walk through the woods on a winter afternoon, except neither of them was dressed for it.

In the clearing in front of them, the two rectangular trailers squatted forty feet apart on cinderblock footings. She pointed to the one with the rusted screen door and missing blind slats. "That's Eric's trailer."

"How do you know?" Po Po asked.

"The other one is way too clean." Raina wiped the moisture off her nose. "Are you sure you don't want my jacket?"

"Will you quit asking? I already said no.

I'm not even cold, and the wet doesn't bother me."

Her grandma was getting snippy, which meant the cold and damp was bothering her. The gray silk pajamas on her grandma blended with their surroundings and would have given her a stealthy ninja look if she were in a movie. As it was, the blue flannel showed through the patches of wet silk and the cane strapped to her waist with a length of cord dragged on the ground, adding to the drowned rat look. Raina would have to trick her grandma into wearing her jacket.

Po Po gripped her cane and looked ready to dash across the clearing. "Let's go."

Twigs snapped and voices drifted over to their hiding spot.

Raina's hand shot out and she grabbed her grandma's arm, pulling her further back into the tree line. "Someone is coming," she whispered.

"I don't hear anything," Po Po whispered back.

Lucille and pool boy Scotty emerged from the fog, his beefy arm slung across her shoulders. Her reddened face could be from the cold or maybe she just had a crying fest. They disappeared into the clean trailer.

Raina's jaw dropped to the floor. For some reason, she'd never linked the two together.

Po Po gave her a gentle shove. "Will you stop gaping like a fool?"

Raina peeled off her jacket and handed it to her grandma. "Here, hold this for me. I'm going in closer."

"I'm coming with you," Po Po whispered back.

Raina shook her head and pointed at the tree several paces in front of them. "That skinny tree is not big enough to hide both of us."

"Why are you giving me your jacket?"

"Um...it makes that plastic sound when it's wet. I don't want them to hear me. You know what, you should put it on. That way your hands are free." Raina mimed a chopping motion. "You never know when you need to make a karate move."

"Okay, girl. I got your back."

Raina left her grandma struggling into her jacket. It was almost as easy as tricking a baby. She hunched low and scrambled toward the skinny tree. Her soaked sneakers squished with each step she took.

Scotty's face appeared in the window.

Raina dropped to the wet ground. Moist leaves and twigs pressed against her cheek. After several heartbeats and with no heavy footsteps coming toward her, she moved her head and peeked at the clearing. Interior light illuminated the gap between the closed blinds and window frame.

Circling the trailer, she looked for an open or uncovered window. No dice. She would have to knock if she wanted to hear what was said between the two.

The rain fell in fat drops. She was soaked to the skin and cold. A drop of rain somehow managed to make its way into the gap on the back of her jeans and rolled down her underwear. She tugged her shirt down, hoping to cover her exposed skin. She made a mental note to check the weather in the future when they do any more skulking.

It was time to pack it in. She didn't want Po Po to catch pneumonia. Maybe they could stop by the police station for news on Brenda and come back later when it stopped raining.

Raina retraced her footsteps to where she'd left her grandma. She scanned the area. "Po Po, come on out."

No answer. Great. Why wasn't her grandma paying attention? If Po Po was behind the oak tree checking her phone...

She rounded the tree and gasped. Her pulse roared inside her ears, and she leaned against the bark for support.

Eric Wagner held Po Po by the collar of the jacket with one hand, and the pimp cane with the other. He glanced up at the sound of her footsteps, and his smile widened.

"Well, if it isn't the Chinese girl with the

Afro. Keep your hands where I can see them." He pointed the cane at her. "I'm not letting you reach for pepper spray or some kind of weapon in your pockets."

Raina held up her hands. She took a deep breath. Calm. She had to stay calm. "I'm reaching for the sky."

Eric frowned as if he had no idea what she meant. "What are you two doing here? Are you planning to rob my home?"

Po Po busted out laughing. "Trust me, big guy. You have nothing that we want."

He shook his hand, causing Po Po to sway and cutting off her laughter.

Raina wanted to smack him, but she knew it wouldn't help their situation. "Does Cecelia know you're boinking Lucille in the utility closet?"

"Leave Lucille out of this," he said through gritted teeth. "Cecelia and I are not together anymore."

Raina gave him a tight smile. Oh, she had his number all right. "That doesn't mean she doesn't like having a tight leash around you. After all, she's your sugar momma. And if she finds out about Lucille, you're going to be out on the streets again. Let my grandma go or I'll make sure she finds out."

His hand tightened on the pimp cane. "Careful, little girl, or I might just make sure you and your grandma end up in the woods where no one can find you."

Raina studied his eyes as they shifted to behind her and then back. Scotty had mentioned arguing with him at the time of Sui Yuk Liang's death. He wasn't the killer, but he was a bully. His type wouldn't stand and fight when challenged.

"I have an email scheduled to hit Cecelia's mailbox in fifteen minutes with all the details of your affair with Lucille and Sui Yuk," Raina said, in a slow and casual tone, lying through her teeth. "It is also cc to my buddy at the police station. If I don't stop the email, well, the butter is going to be missing from your gravy train."

"You're bluffing," Eric said, his eyes shifting to his trailer. "You can't do stuff like that."

Po Po pulled out her cell phone and waved it under his nose. "Not only can you schedule an email, but I can transfer money around the world with this. Geez, don't you keep up with the times?"

He flushed. "I embrace simple living. I don't have fancy gizmos."

"In other words, your sugar mama—"

Raina cleared her throat. "Sorry to interrupt the love fest. But do we really want Cecelia to know about Eric's side dish?"

Eric released Po Po, but held on to the pimp cane. "I need a beer." He stomped past Raina toward his trailer, swinging the cane back and forth at the brown brush on the ground.

Po Po trotted next to him, looking like a Chihuahua yipping at a Doberman. "I want my cane back."

He ignored her, yanked open his screen

door, and stalked inside his home. Po Po followed him, reaching for the door handle.

Raina grabbed her hand. "How do you
know he doesn't have an axe in there? You
know—axe murderer."

"My underwear is soaked. My socks gush
water every step I take. I'm freezing." Po Po
opened the screen door. "You can stay out
here if you want, but I'm going in."

Raina glanced at Scotty's trailer. Someone
had turned off the light as if the inhabitants
were waiting. She hoped this wasn't a mistake,
and plunged in after her grandma.

21

THE COVER-UP

The trailer was much neater than she'd expected and surprisingly more festive. A three-foot Christmas tree rested on a folding table with three chairs in one corner. A trail of wadded wrapping papers led from the table to the trashcan in the kitchenette. The closed doorway probably opened to his bedroom.

Eric was sprawled on his recliner, one leg thrown over the armrest. A framed photo of three smiling girls rested on the small side table next to him. He gestured with his beer can toward the floor. The thin rug had more stains than beige. His mom must be proud of his hospitality.

He studied them from his throne like they were his subjects. "What do you want? There's nothing here that you can possibly want." Then he grinned. "Unless you want me to show you a good time."

"Ewww! I should smack you for making such a disgusting proposition," Po Po said. "I'd rather pick my nose. Now where's my cane?"

"Not you, old bat—"

"Those are fighting words. Do you want a piece of me? I can give it to you again, you old goat—"

"You caught me unawares. And I don't go around beating little old ladies—"

"I'm not old. We're practically the same age—"

"You have at least twenty years on me—"

"Do not! Check my license. I'm only sixty—"

Raina stuck two fingers in her mouth and

whistled. "Look, I hate to break up the make-out session, but the email is going to hurl through cyberspace in a few minutes. Let's get this show on the road."

"He called me old—"

"There's a seat for you in the car," Raina said.

Po Po harrumphed and crossed her arms.

Eric slouched lower on the recliner. "I don't have to talk to you."

"I haven't told the police you tried kidnapping Sui Yuk Liang's baby outside of Bullseye." Raina paused. "But I could."

His face darkened. "Well, someone sure did. The police came by yesterday. I was in the middle of opening Christmas presents with my kids."

Raina widened her eyes in pretend surprise. "Maybe a good Samaritan turned you in. Why would you want to jeopardize"—she gestured around the trailer—"this by attempting to kidnap the baby?"

"I don't have a high school diploma, but I

understand sarcasm. I was rescuing the child like Sui Yuk would have wanted. How do you think my phone number got into the diaper bag in the first place?"

"You probably put it in the bag yourself," Po Po said.

"Did not," Eric said.

"Did to."

Raina clapped her hands. "Children, can we please focus? You're right. You don't have to talk to me. But good luck explaining to the police how you got the extortion money from Sui Yuk's husband."

"Stop twisting my words. It was a reward for securing the safety of his son until he could get someone to collect the child. A man has to have a contingency plan. I can't live off of Cece forever. My youngest will be in high school the next year, and she'll have no use for an on-call babysitter then."

Now it was Raina's turn to study Eric. She didn't figure he would be a family man.

"If he's so concerned about his son, why isn't he here with his wife?" Po Po asked.

"Because Sui Yuk is his mistress. His wife is from a rich and powerful family in China, but she couldn't have kids. And he wanted a son. Somehow he is convinced his wife would be onboard to raise the baby as theirs. But from what little I know about women, he's delusional. What wife would want to have breakfast with her husband's bastard?"

Po Po blanched, and her face became a closed shop.

Raina slid a sideways glance at her grandma. Her stomach lurched at the hummingbirds crashing around in there. "Do you think his wife might have known about the affair?" She refocused on Eric, so she could pretend not to see her grandma studying her.

"Oh, the wife knows. She visited Sui Yuk at the condo owned by the husband. Apparently he also kept his previous mistress there. The wife said she'd turn a blind eye as long as Sui Yuk didn't produce a child."

"But there is a child," Po Po whispered, her voice harsh and flat.

"Is the baby even Sui Yuk's?" Raina asked, still afraid to look at her grandma. "I heard she had a stillbirth, left the resort, and came back with a baby a month later."

Eric shrugged. "Sui Yuk said the baby was hers."

"But why come back to the resort? Why not leave immediately for China?"

"I have no idea. The husband pre-paid for two months post-partum. I guess she didn't want to waste the money."

"What if Sui Yuk did have a stillbirth? Cecelia's questionable business practices set her up for blackmail. Could she have stolen another woman's baby to placate Sui Yuk?"

"Play—what?"

"To get Sui Yuk off her—"

"Hey, you okay?" Eric asked Po Po. He swung his leg off the armrest. "Your cane is behind the front door."

Her grandma swayed as if she stood before a gusty wind.

Raina reached for Po Po's arm, but her grandma lurched away from her. Eric dropped his beer can and caught her grandma before she hit the floor.

Po Po's eyes fluttered like fragile butterfly wings against her ashen cheeks.

"Hey, are you okay? Should I call an ambulance?" Eric asked gently.

Raina kneeled next to her grandma. "Po Po? Can you hear me?"

"I'm fine. I want to go home."

"Okay. Let me help you up."

Po Po jerked her arm, twisting her body away from Raina. "I don't need your help. Young man, give me a hand."

Eric flicked his eyes at Raina and heaved Po Po up by the armpits. "I'll give you a ride back to your car on my golf cart."

The rain had stopped, but Raina's underwear was still damp. Po Po sat up front with Eric, her back stiff and ramrod straight. She didn't say anything further to either one of them. Eric stopped the golf cart next to the faded Honda Accord.

"I need to get back to work," Eric said as they climbed out. He hightailed it out of the parking lot without further ado.

The short ride back to the senior condo complex was silent. The similarity of Sui Yuk Liang's situation to Ah Gong's secret family in China was too coincidental. The ancestors were telling her something, but Raina had a feeling she missed it.

A small part of her squirmed with guilt for keeping Sui Yuk Liang's concubine status from her grandma. But another part of her felt oddly protective of the young mom. She had no friends and no money of her own. Most women wouldn't choose such a life unless they had no other options. Being the mistress to one man was better than being the mistress to many men.

"Just drop me off. I can get up by myself,"

Po Po said, interrupting her thoughts. "There's no need to park."

Raina parked and ran to open the door for her grandma. Po Po swept out of the car like a grand dame, and Raina was nothing more than the hired help for the notice she was given. The elevator dinged, and they stepped inside. Raina was beginning to wonder if she should just leave when her grandma spoke.

"You knew all along Sui Yuk Liang was a home wrecker," Po Po said, thumping her cane to give emphasis to her words. "I can't believe you want to help someone like her."

Raina hesitated. She didn't want to antagonize her grandma further. "She doesn't deserve to die."

"You lied to me again."

"I was protecting you. I knew you would react—"

"I don't need your protection. And I don't need you."

Raina wrapped her arms around her body, tucking her trembling hands into her armpits. "Po Po?" Her voice came out in a strained whisper. She cleared her throat. "Justice sometimes needs a little nudge to balance its scale. Don't you believe this anymore? If Sui Yuk had a choice, why would she choose to be at the beck and call of a rich man?"

Her grandma averted her gaze. "Sometimes the scale is too out of balance for a simple nudge. What about the poor wife sitting at home? Does she deserve to have her life explode on her?"

Raina licked her lips, and replied carefully, "I think both women are victims. If anyone has to take the blame, I blame the husband."

"Then why were you so quick to cover up for your granddad?"

The elevator door opened. Maggie Louie stood in the hall, waiting to get in. They stepped out, and Po Po exchanged a quick word with her best friend. Maggie sneaked a quick look at Raina, but got into the elevator even though it was clear she could see Po Po was upset.

Po Po made her way to her condo, her cane thumping louder than it needed to be on the carpet. Raina cringed at the muffled noise but trotted after her grandma. The last time she'd seen her grandma this upset was when Po Po got kicked off the board from the family shipping company after Ah Gong's death. Her grandma opened the front door and stalked in.

On the sofa, Fanny painted her toenails with the concentration of a brain surgeon. She greeted Po Po, nodded at Raina, and returned to setting the rhinestone on her big toe. It must be a wonder to have so little care in this world.

Po Po stalked into her bedroom, throwing her cane onto the bed. She pulled pajamas from the dresser drawer.

Raina flopped down on the bed, like she'd done a thousand times before.

"Get off the bed. You're going to get the

sheets wet," Po Po snapped. "Why are you still here?"

Raina hopped off the bed like her pants were on fire. "What happened to always being on my team?"

"We're only on the same team when we're playing in the same field. I'm tired of second-guessing your motives. I don't trust you anymore."

Raina flushed at her sudden flash of anger. Her skin felt too tight for her body. "Is this why you wouldn't let me tell the rest of the family about Ah Gong's secret? Are you punishing me for your husband's infidelity?"

"I thought your loyalty lies with me."

"Like you always say, you're asking me which toe to cut off. It was his dying wish. Do I think it was wrong? Yes. But I took on this shackle for you."

"Oh, please. You just wanted the money."

Raina whispered, "I've struggled with this burden. I've given up my friends and family to give you time to come to terms with your husband's death. You wouldn't have been able to handle his infidelity on top of everything else..." Her voice broke, and she swallowed the lump in her throat. "And this is the thanks I get—from you and from everyone else."

"I could handle the truth. I'm not a child."

Raina shook her head. "You're not the only victim in this family drama. Either we work together to move past this, or I'm leaving you behind."

Po Po took a deep breath. "You need to leave. I don't want to say something I might regret later."

As Raina fled the bedroom, a tear rolled down her cheek. Fanny gave her a quizzical look, but she ignored the foreign exchange student and kept going until she got into the elevator. She pressed her trembling lips together. If she gave in to the tears, she wouldn't be able to stop until she collapsed into a wet puddle.

At the lobby, two women chatted about the upcoming New Year's Eve party. One of the women opened her mouth as if to speak, but Raina strolled through the double doors to the Senior Center's Rec Room.

Frank Small, her best friend Eden's grand-dad, sat by the police scanner. He waved for her to come over, but Raina shook her head and headed toward the reading chairs facing the windows of the courtyard.

He marched over and stood in front of her. "Raina, we need to talk. It's about your grandmother."

22

THE ROOF IS ON FIRE

Raina clenched and unclenched her jaw. The last thing she wanted was to make small talk when she could sit in the dark and count the flashing lightning outside. She blinked at the burning behind her eyes, and another tear rolled down.

Before she was even conscious of her decision, Raina bawled on Frank's shoulder and told him the entire sob story about the investigation and its impact on her relationship with her grandma.

She hiccupped and swiped at the tears on

her face. "How did everything come out so wrong? I had good intentions. Po Po acted as if she was fine."

Frank patted her hand. "This would have come to a head sooner or later. You're her favorite granddaughter. Don't you think she has every right to feel betrayed by you?"

Raina nodded reluctantly. Lying by omission was still lying. If she were in her grandma's shoes, not only would she feel betrayed, but her pride would also take a huge bruising for not suspecting anything was amiss in her marriage. With her husband gone, there wasn't anyone else to direct this anger toward. "I still don't understand how such a family man could hide this secret for so many years."

"Maybe being a family man was his downfall. It could have been a mistake from his youth, and he took responsibility for it all these years. It didn't mean he loved his wife or his family any less."

Raina tilted her head, considering his words. She could imagine Ah Gong taking on a life sentence for a mistake in his twenties. Family meant everything to her grandfather, especially since he'd survived his parents and siblings by the time he was a teen.

"I wish I'd never agreed to take Fanny shopping last Saturday," Raina said. "Things could've turned out differently if she didn't miss the bus. Maybe Po Po and I would have talked about it instead of letting it explode like this."

Frank frowned. "It broke down in front of the Town Hall that morning. Mayor Goodwin suggested it was a terrorist attack, but the police chief ignored him." He pointed at the police scanner across the room. "Donna put out the APB, but no one took it seriously. The mayor used the slow response time as an example of why Gold Springs needs the agreement with the sheriff in the briefing later in the afternoon. Don't you watch the news?"

"Not really. Between the gossip from Po Po and what Eden tells me, I know everything there is to know."

Frank grunted in disgust. He mumbled something unflattering about young people and the drain.

The police scanner crackled, and Raina jumped at the noise.

...fire... Wellness Lane...

Frank crossed the room, fiddled with a knob, and the static faded out.

By the end of the dispatch, Raina clutched her car keys. Things were certainly coming to a head tonight. "I need to go. The fire is at the Women Wellness and Birth Clinic."

As RAINA DROVE to the resort, she wondered if she needed backup. If they were still on the same team, she would have asked Po Po to join her. With all the police and firefighters on the scene, she doubted the killer would strike, but it never hurt to have someone watching her back.

While there was no evidence the killer

was the same person who had broken into her apartment, it made her jumpy all the same. Anonymity while snooping around was her greatest protection. Now someone put her under a microscope. And after the fiasco with her grandma, she couldn't help but second-guess her decisions.

She glanced at the clock on her dashboard. A little after eight. Her stomach rumbled, reminding her the last time she ate was several hours ago. She didn't expect to be much help at the scene, so a quick look-see and then off to the drive-thru.

The acrid smoke came in through the air vents before the tree-lined road opened out to the parking lot of the birth clinic. Vehicles were strewn haphazardly in front of the cottage-style building hidden among the trees. She pulled over to the side, making sure the Accord wouldn't be in anyone's way. The last thing she wanted was for a fire truck to total her car.

She jogged over to the ring of onlookers

on the edge of the action. Flames and smoke rolled out the broken windows. The west wing of the roof looked ready to collapse. If the fire had started half an hour earlier, the rain would have helped to reduce the flames. As it was, the fine mist added to the general irritation of soot and bits of paper floating around.

"Is there anyone inside?" Raina asked the man next to her. Her throat was already coated with grime from breathing the astringent air.

"No," he said, glancing down at her. Dale Sprint, Eden's rival at the newspaper office, recognized her the instant she placed him. "The patients return to their suites after labor and delivery." His eyes lit with an inner fire. "I can't believe I've never heard about the goings-on at this place. This article would make the chief reconsider Eden's promotion."

Raina's heart sank. Her best friend Eden would be a caged tiger once he published a column on the birth resort. She could see the byline now—the new gold rush, citizenships for sale. The fallout wouldn't be pretty for Eden or their town.

Dale flicked a curl off his blue eyes. "Is Eden asking you to spy on me? Whatever she's paying you, I'll match it." He stepped closer. His eyes darkened into a sooty come-hither look. "I can definitely beat it. How about dinner sometime?"

Raina would rather chew her own leg off. She looked around the crowd. Toni watched them by the big redwood tree. "I need to go." She made her way to the private investigator while dodging other lookie-loos who had a few hours to kill on a Saturday night.

"Have you located Muyang yet?" Raina asked.

Toni sighed, rubbing a hand over her face. "She was caught red-handed inside the building. The police handcuffed her and stuffed her into the back of the cruiser." She jerked her thumb at the vehicle with an officer speaking into his walkie talkie. "They'll bring her back to the station for questioning later."

"Was she holding some kind of flame accelerant? Why would she set fire to the place? This makes no sense."

"I don't know, and I no longer care. Muyang is getting her retainer back with my blessing. I'll call around for a lawyer, but that's it. I can't work for someone who won't take my advice and would rather run around like a loose cannon."

"Why did you take her case in the first place?"

"I'm a sucker for a good sob story. Muyang had no friends and no money, and she claimed someone stole her newborn baby. Her husband couldn't come because they used their last yuan to send her here. They wanted their son to get a head start in life with a U.S. citizenship. I'm a grandma myself, so I fell for it—hook, line, and sinker."

Raina stared at the police vehicle parked fifty feet away. A shadow moved in the dark interior of the backseat. The similarity between Sui Yuk and Muyang was eerie. Only one of them was BL's mother, but which one? "For what it's worth, I don't believe she would start the fire. This could destroy the evidence she seeks."

Toni pulled a cell phone from her jacket pocket. "I have to make phone calls. We'll catch up later?"

Raina nodded and watched the private investigator disappear into the night. She scanned the scene in front of her, but other than Dale Sprint, she recognized no one else. Her stomach rumbled again.

If she went through the drive-thru, she should have time to grab the frozen cheesecake in her apartment and get to the police station as they bring in Muyang. With such a treat, the front desk clerk would discreetly give Raina the inside scoop on the arrest.

The cell phone in her jeans pocket vibrated. She pulled out a condom along with her phone. Extra lube for her pleasure. She rolled her eyes as she stuffed it back into her pocket. It'd only been a few hours, but she already missed Po Po.

She tapped on the broken screen, opening the text message from a number she didn't recognize. Her heart stopped, and blood pounded inside her ears. The phone slipped out of her numb hands and shattered on the ground.

COME TO **STE 18** ALONE. I HAVE YOUR GRANDMA AND SISTER.

23

LIGHTS OUT

Someone touched Raina's elbow, and she shrieked. Several people glanced at her direction and returned their attention to the fire.

"Hey, calm down," Dale said, holding out the broken pieces of her cell phone. "You okay?"

Raina knew panic wouldn't help her grandma. She took a deep breath, but ended up coughing from the smoke. Her face grew hotter as she wasted precious seconds trying to stop hacking so she could speak. "Help."

Her voice came out in a weak whisper. "Someone kidnapped my grandma. Suite Eighteen."

"Calm down. Follow my lead," Dale said, inhaling and exhaling. "In and out. You need oxygen."

Someone called out to the news reporter, and he turned his attention away from her.

She grabbed his arm, squeezing it to get his attention. "Tell the police there's a kidnapping in progress. Suite Eighteen."

Dale yelped. "Hey, stop that." He jerked his arm away from her grasp.

Raina backed away from him. Useless. "Find Detective Matthew Louie. Kidnapping. Suite Eighteen." She turned and ran toward the walking trail that connected the clinic to the rest of the resort.

In the daylight this path was a vision of laughter and light. Flowers and ivory weaved themselves around the wood trellises. In the dark, the lattices created more shadows that mimicked the fear in her heart.

With Muyang in the back of the police cruiser, who else would have a reason to kidnap her grandma? Obviously, the person got to her at the condo since they'd managed to take Fanny too.

Is the kidnapper the same person who killed Sui Yuk? Cecelia or Eric? It had to be one of them, but which one?

Her breaths came out in labored puffs. Though the distance to Suite Eighteen was shorter than her morning runs, the terrain was much rougher. The dim moonlight lent the ground a flatness it didn't normally have. She stumbled on a rock and almost fell over.

The back of Suite Eighteen appeared in front of her. The interior was dark, and Raina slowed. No point in announcing her presence to the killer yet. Surprise was her only advantage. She crept up to the window and peered into the bedroom. The door was closed, but the strip of light at the bottom acted as a beacon. Everyone was in the living room.

She tried the window, but it was locked.

The bathroom window was too small, which meant she would have to go in through the front door or the patio door. Since they were side by side up front, what difference did it make which door she chose? The killer would be waiting for her on the other side.

What if this was a trap? What if her grandma was asleep in her bed, dreaming of sugarplums and dancing bears in tutus?

Cecelia or Eric? One would lose the resort, and the other his sugar mama. What if they were in on this together? They had a lot to lose if Sui Yuk were able to turn over evidence of Cecelia's questionable business practices. Both of them would lose their livelihoods.

What choice did she have? Her grandma and Fanny were inside. All she could do was hold the killer off until the police showed up. She had to believe Dale would talk to an officer. Even the cast of *Mission Impossible* had more to work with than a key card and condom.

Raina gripped the knob and swiped the

key card. She dropped into a tackling position and rushed into the room, hoping for a second of surprise to do some damage. The room was emptied, except for Fanny and Po Po. They were tied up like pigs on a stick on the floor.

"Hurry," Fanny mumbled over the gag in her mouth. Her frightened eyes shifted to the doorway behind Raina. "He went out looking for you. He'll be back any minute."

Raina spun and closed the door. She flipped the security lock above the keycard lock. It might not be much, but at least it would give her a warning when Eric returned.

Po Po jerked and made muffled noises. Her eyebrows twitched up and down as if they were possessed.

Raina rushed over to her, working on the knots on her grandma's hands. "You can be mad at me later."

The only warning she got was a rustling noise, and pain radiated from the back of her neck. The room spun in a slow circle. She reached out to grab onto something, and her face hit the carpeted floor.

Someone grunted. Angry mumbling in Chinese.

Raina cracked open watery eyes to see Fanny crouched in front of her. She reached for her head, but stopped short. Her hands were bound behind her. She shifted her eyes.

Po Po sobbed, tears dripping into the dirty gag and onto the carpet. Drip. Drip. The wet spot spread on the carpet next to the pimp cane.

Raina closed her eyes, willing away the fog. She needed to have her wits. Someone kicked her legs, and the pain raced up her back. She blinked at the tears, but at least she could focus now.

Fanny hovered over her. How did she get out of her ties?

Raina stared at her in confusion for half a heartbeat. Her hands were never tied in the first place. It was all a ruse. The foreign exchange student killed Sui Yuk.

"Why?" Raina mumbled, pretending to be less coherent than she actually was. "Did you hate my grandma's cooking this much?" She tugged against the restraint. There was enough slack to get her wrists out if she could get some butter on them.

Fanny's expression was cold and impersonal. Even the pink highlights in her hair made her face appear harder than normal with the shadows from the cheap overhanging light. "I didn't want to, but she made me do it when she decided to have my husband's baby. Our arrangement was for Sui Yuk Liang to keep my husband happy so I no longer had to share a bed with him. But a baby? That changes everything."

Raina tugged at the rope again, wincing at the burning pain around her wrist. This wasn't going to work. "What happened to looking for a rich American husband?"

"It was a contingency plan in case things didn't work out."

Raina shuddered. She couldn't imagine

making such a marriage. It was better being alone than to be lonely in a crowd. She pulled the condom out of her back pocket and continued talking as she tore the crackling wrapper open. "Ever hear of divorce? I can't believe you have an arrangement with your husband's mistress?" She unrolled the rubber, smearing the lubricant on her wrists with her fingers. Tugging and rotating, she finally got her hands out of the rope.

"Not everything is about love," Fanny said, dragging out the word love. She gave Raina a pitying look as if she were a naive child. "But the whore thought she could replace me because she can give him the child that I can't. There is no way he would divorce me. I am his ultimate trophy wife. Without the political connections from my family, his tiny shoe factory wouldn't have gotten the government contracts."

"So you killed Sui Yuk because you're jealous she could get pregnant?"

Fanny snorted. "What do I care about children? No, I killed her because she defied me. She thought she could replace me."

Po Po's eyes tracked Raina's movement. "Good for you. If I could do the same with my husband's mistress, I would run her over myself. But you created a lot of trouble for the Sullivans."

Fanny shrugged at Po Po. "I'm sorry you and the Sullivans were caught in this. I have a four o'clock flight back to China. You two only need to stay here until then. The maid will set you free in the morning."

Raina patted the ground until she made contact with the condom. "Hey!"

Fanny glanced over. "What? You can be so annoying sometimes."

Raina swung her hands in front of her, hooked the opening of the condom to her thumb, and slingshot it onto Fanny's face.

As Fanny swatted at the slippery raincoat, her face twisted into a snarl. "Ugh."

Raina lunged for the pimp cane, but Fanny grabbed the other end.

"You have defied me for the last time, Raina," she said through clenched teeth.

"You're probably right." Raina pushed the balls on the horse statue.

The lower jaw of the horse slid down. A jet of pea-green liquid squirted out between its teeth and into Fanny's mouth. Skunk funk immediately dispersed into the air.

Fanny gagged, dry heaving as tears ran down her face. She stumbled back and tripped over Po Po's bound legs.

Raina swung the cane at Fanny, and it was lights out for the killer.

She swallowed the bile in the back of her throat and kneeled next to her grandma. She kept an eye on Fanny while she worked at the knots on her grandma's hands. Her breaths came out in loud huffs as she breathed through her mouth.

Bam! Bam!

Raina's heart leapt to her throat, and she bit the inside of her cheek to stop herself from shrieking. She grabbed the cane and swung around.

The door flew open, and bits of the doorframe sailed in their direction. Matthew and two other officers ran into the room with guns drawn. His gaze flicked from Raina to Fanny's still body on the floor.

"Does he always show up after all the action is over?" Po Po whispered into her ear.

Raina nodded. "Pretty much."

"I never had much use for a man who came late."

Raina snorted, more in appreciation for her grandma's attempt to lighten the mood than actual mirth. Her white-knuckle grip on the cane was the only thing keeping her hands from shaking.

While the two police officers went to secure the suite, Matthew came over. "Where is Eric?"

"He had nothing to do with Sui Yuk Liang's death." Raina pointed at Fanny. "She's the murderer."

24

TIME TO REDECORATE

A week later, as Raina was getting ready for her date, there was a knock on the door. She glanced at the time displayed on her new cell phone. Much too early for Blue's arrival. She ignored it and continued using the flat iron on her curly hair. If it was Po Po, she could use her key. And if it was someone else, her hair was more important at the moment.

"I know you are in there, Rainy," Matthew called out.

Raina turned off the flat iron and trudged

to the door. She flung it open but positioned her body so he couldn't see the mess in her living room.

Matthew eyed her hair. "Are you busy? I thought you might be interested in what we found out about Fanny."

"I'm not interested in Fanny. I already know too much as it is," Raina said. "Who started the fire?"

"Cecelia was shredding her second set of books when Muyang broke into the clinic. Fearing it was the private investigator snooping around the resort, Cecelia dumped everything in the trash, along with her cigarette, and emptied a bottle of rose perfume on top of it."

"She's lucky she didn't kill herself or someone else. Did she finally admit to kidnapping a baby for Sui Yuk?"

"No, and the doctor is conveniently visiting her family in the Philippines."

"So Cecelia is off the hook?"

"A package of evidence showed up at the

DA's office a couple days after the fire. I have no idea who it's from, but there's enough there to put Cecelia away for a good while."

Raina thought about Toni Moody snooping around the resort. She wasn't the only one who cared about doing the right thing. "What about BL? Is he still in foster care?"

"The judge expedited a DNA test. Muyang is being reunited with her son even as we speak."

Raina smiled at the sudden weight lifting from her chest. She hadn't realized how much she still worried about the child. "This is wonderful news." She started to close the door. "Thanks for coming by, but I need to get back to what I'm doing."

He glanced above her head and frowned. "What happened to the koi clock I got you for your graduation?"

Raina had hoped he wouldn't notice. "I'm redecorating."

He studied her, his lips pressed into a thin line, for several heartbeats. "Good for you."

She gave him a wobbly smile. "It's good to start something new."

"We never got a chance to finish that conversation of ours at the cafe."

"It's okay, Matthew. I understand now."

He frowned. "You do?"

She nodded. "It would make life easier if we don't spend time together."

"I'm perfectly fine with the way things are."

"I'm sure you are. But I don't have your self-control. If you want to help me out, let's not bring sexy back."

"Not even just for fun?"

Raina shook her head. "No offense, but I'm looking elsewhere for my fun. I need closure, and I can't get it when you're always around."

Matthew stiffened. "So this is it?"

"Yes. You have been telling me this for years, and I'm finally listening."

"What convinced you?"

"When I saw you with my cousins at the Christmas party. The Wongs are family in a way yours never was. I get it."

"I'm sorry your grandma left town."

Raina cleared her throat. "It's just temporarily. It's not like she sold the condo."

Matthew studied her face as if imprinting it in his memory. He gave her a sad smile. "Stay out of trouble, Rainy. See you around."

Raina leaned forward and gave him a quick peck on the cheek. "I hope not."

She closed the door and leaned against it. She swallowed the knot in her throat and blinked at the burning in her eyes. Blue would be here in fifteen minutes for their date. She still had half a head of hair to straighten. This was no time to cry over what might have been.

THE END

PLEASE REVIEW my books at your retailer. As an indie author, reviews help other readers find my books. I appreciate all reviews, whether positive or negative.

Continue Raina's story now.
Breezy Friends and Bodies
(Raina Sun #3)

ALSO BY ANNE R. TAN

Thanks for reading *Gusty Lovers and Cadavers.* I hope you enjoyed it!

Did you like this book?

Please review my books at your *retailer*. As an indie author, reviews help other readers find my books. I appreciate all reviews, whether positive or negative.

Want to know about new releases, sale pricing, and exclusive content?

Sign up for Anne R. Tan's email newsletter at http://annertan.com/newsletter

Your information would not be sold or transferred. Thank you for trusting me with your email.

Want More Raina Sun?

Gusty Lovers and Cadavers (Raina Sun #2)

Breezy Friends and Bodies (Raina Sun #3)

Balmy Darlings and Death (Raina Sun #4)

Sunny Mates and Murders (Raina Sun #5)

Murky Passions and Scandals (Raina Sun #6)

Smoldering Flames and Secrets (Raina Sun #7)

Hazy Grooms and Homicides (Raina Sun #8)

Chilly Comforts and Disasters (Raina Sun #9)

Fair Cronies and Felonies (Raina Sun Mystery #10)

How about another series by Anne R. Tan?

Just Shoot Me Dead (Lucy Fong #1)

Just Lost and Found (Lucy Fong #1.5)

Just a Lucy Break-In (Lucy Fong #2)

ABOUT THE AUTHOR

Anne R. Tan is a *USA Today* bestselling author. She writes the Raina Sun Mystery series and the Lucy Fong Mystery series. Her humorous cozy mysteries feature Chinese-American amateur sleuths dealing with love, family, and life while solving murders.

Sign up for her newsletter for new release announcement, sales, and exclusive content at http://annertan.com/newsletter/

A NOTE FROM ANNE:

My books are my legacy to my children. Unfortunately, they won't grow up in the San Francisco Bay Area as I did. Without a cultural hub to keep the language and philosophies alive, our family will lose this part of our heritage in one generation. My children will be visitors to this rich culture just like my readers. I hope you'll enjoy your time with Raina Sun and her large dynamic family.

9 781952 317002